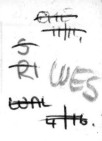

Shame in the Blood

Shame in the Blood

a novel

by Tetsuo Miura

Translated by Andrew Driver

All stories originally published in
Japanese by Shinchosha, Tokyo.
"A Portrait of Shino (Shinobugawa)"
and "Shame in the Blood (Haji no fu)"
appeared in *Shinobugawa,* published
in 1961. "Face of Death (Shoya)" and
"Magic Lantern Show (Gento gashu)"
appeared in *Shoya,* published in 1961.
"Homecoming (Kikyo)" and "*And All
Promenade!* (Danran)" appeared in
Danran, published in 1964. All rights
reserved.

Cover design by Kimberly Glyder
Interior design by Gopa & Ted2, Inc.

*This book has been selected by the
Japanese Literature Publishing Project
(JLPP) which is run by the Japanese
Literature Publishing and Promotion
Center (J-Lit Center) on behalf of the
Agency for Cultural Affairs of Japan.*

ISBN-13: 978-1-59376-189-9
ISBN-10: 1-59376-189-9

SHOEMAKER HOARD

www.shoemakerhoard.com

9 8 7 6 5 4 3 2 1

Contents

# A Portrait of Shino

I ONCE TOOK SHINO to Fukagawa in the old part of Tokyo. It was not long after we'd first met.

Fukagawa was where Shino was born and had lived until the age of twelve. I myself had only arrived in Tokyo from the remote north of Tohoku the previous spring, and it was strange to think that I should now be taking this "Fukagawan" back to the place of her birth. But Shino had been evacuated to Tochigi the summer before the war ended and had never since returned to Fukagawa, which had been razed to the ground and would now be quite unrecognizable to her. Whereas I, a kid from the countryside, was in the habit of walking through Fukagawa two or three times a month, sometimes even on consecutive Sundays. To me, Fukagawa was the most familiar neighborhood in the whole of Tokyo, excluding my route to and from the university each day.

We took a tram that passed through Fukagawa on its way from Kinshibori to Tokyo Station, and got off in front of Fukagawa

Toyo Park, at the corner where the tramlines met the Susaki Canal and made an abrupt ninety-degree turn. As the tram moved off, Shino stretched her back, inhaling the air, and surveyed the streets around us. It was a hot sunny day in July. With their rows of squat, makeshift houses baking in the blazing sun, the streets smoldered with white dust and shimmering heat.

"Oh dear. It's completely different," Shino said forlornly. "I feel like a stranger here. The only thing I remember is the school."

She pointed across the road toward a three-storey building whose charred concrete hulk was exposed to the sun. That building had been Shino's school for five years.

"Don't worry," I said. "It'll come back to you as we go along. After all, you *were* born and raised here, weren't you?"

Shino laughed. "That's right. Well, everything else may have changed, but at least the roads should be the same." She returned her gaze to the gutted school building. "It's just that . . . well, I'd heard the whole place had been burned to the ground, but I couldn't imagine that the school would burn, too. I just couldn't believe that a concrete building would go up in flames like that. But as soon as I saw it, I realized it was true, because of the windows. When a concrete building burns, the windows all turn black, don't they."

I watched her as she looked across at the blackened windows, pressed together like honeycomb cells whose edges had been burned away. When she blinked her thin almond eyes as if she'd made some unexpected discovery, it was my turn to laugh.

"Well, if you get distracted like this each time, we'll be here all day!"

Shino shrugged her shoulders. "All right, will you lead the way? Which is closer, I wonder."

"I'd say Kiba."

"I would have thought Susaki."

Susaki, as I recalled, lay on the other side of the canal. In that case we could walk there from Kiba. And so it was that Shino and I crossed the shimmering tramlines, passed through the long, narrow shadow cast over the road by Shino's old school, and headed toward the reservoirs at Kiba.

Shino wanted to visit the place where I'd last seen my brother. And while we were there, she would show me where she had been born and raised.

Kiba is a district of timber and canals. Whenever I went there, the wind was strong, and the water in the reservoirs was constantly ruffled by the waves rippling beneath the floating rafts. The wind at Kiba carried the fragrance of wood and the smell of drainwater. It was thick with sawdust that stung the eyes of the uninitiated like smoke from a bonfire; the only ones who walked through Kiba with tears in their eyes were people from other parts of the country.

The first time I walked through Kiba, I had also cried, much to the amusement of my brother, who had taken me there. Yes, my heart was bursting with joy that we should be walking side by side. But if there were tears in my eyes, the wind was surely to blame.

And the spring before, returning to Tokyo for the first time in two years, I had again walked through Kiba. My brother had already left our lives by then, and my heart must have been burning with a kind of rage. But even then it was the wind, I was sure, that persistently clouded my vision. Perhaps my eyes would never get used to Kiba. Or perhaps, in all of Kiba, the sawdust was particularly thick on the route I always took. In any case, I'd long since abandoned hope of ever getting used to it.

On this day, however, Kiba was different, its atmosphere strangely remote. The piles of wood, the reservoirs, everything was bathed in an oddly dazzling light that seemed to deflect my gaze, and even the sound of saws slicing through wood seemed utterly alien to my ears. I had come to know a few faces on my now-customary walks—the old woman in the cigarette shop, the delivery boy at the noodle restaurant, the guards outside the row of lumber mills, the truck drivers. For some time after I had lost my brother, I would go around asking about him, his old pocket notebook in hand, hoping to discover something of his fate. Those good people all mistook me for a detective at first, only to break into the broadest of smiles later. But on this day, for some reason, they simply stared at us with odd looks in their eyes. When I looked back at them, they would abruptly turn away or issue strange groaning sounds. And my eyes were dry from beginning to end. Perhaps even the wind was avoiding me today.

It was as if Kiba didn't know me when I felt happiness in my heart.

Shino and I stood together beside a reservoir on the outskirts of Kiba. The wind blew straight into our faces, and sunlight crashing on the water quivered and glinted endlessly on its surface. Two or three rafts floated in the distance. Behind them, a mass of timber refuse stretched out drearily into the distance, and, beyond that, I could hear the sound of unfamiliar machinery, like the droning of horseflies.

"This is as far as we go. Well, that's Kiba for you. There's nothing here at all," I said, spitting out over the water.

"What a nice breeze. It's as if I've come home to Fukagawa at last."

Under a blazing sun, I had led Shino this way and that around these streets, which felt foreign even to me. Yet she happily turned her little face toward the breeze, while loose strands of hair clung to the perspiration on her forehead and cheeks.

"Let's go home. You must be bored," I said. I regretted taking her there.

She shook her head as if to disagree. "No, no, we've just gotten here. Let's stay a little while longer."

She squatted down with her arms around her chest. "Is this it?" she asked simply.

"Yes," I replied.

That was where I'd last seen my brother. He had studied applied chemistry at technical college and had gone to make torpedoes at the Naval Department's Explosives Research Institute. But after the war, for some reason known only to him, he had joined the lumber company that owned this reservoir. When he handed me his business card I noticed that he was already a "managing director." He worked with that company for five years, and had been there for four years when I graduated from senior high school back home and came to Tokyo. I started university with his financial support. I was the youngest of six children, and our father was already getting on in years. Even so, my brother didn't seem to find me too burdensome. Whenever I needed money, I would just go to his company and ask him for some. He would nonchalantly hand me the cash each time, then treat me to some hearty meal, like a *yanagawa-nabe* stew. A year later, in early spring, I went to see my brother again. We hadn't met in a while. In the deserted office, an old man was warming himself at a brazier. He said that the managing director was not at his desk, but might be out on the reservoir. I passed through the silence of the factory and went up to the edge of the reservoir. The wind still held a wintry chill and created furrows on the surface of the water. The water was translucent all the way to the bottom. My brother, alone, was stepping restively from raft to raft, holding a fireman's hook pole without making particular use of it. The sight of him in his white shirt, without his jacket on, was almost dazzling. It gave me a kind of start. Instinctively, I called his name. He stopped still in a faltering pose, then slowly moved across to the raft nearest the shore. I ran along the concrete edge of the reservoir toward the point nearest the raft, but the distance that separated us across the water must still have been forty feet or more. "What is it?" he shouted, perching precariously on the edge of the raft. I shouted back that it was just the usual request for money. Right away he nodded and said I was to take the bank passbook and the name seal from the office drawer. I should use as much as I needed. He had other business to attend to that day, so we should meet another time. For a little while, we just stared at each other in silence. With the setting sun behind him, my brother seemed taller than usual. His sunken eyes formed large, dark shadows that made his head look like a skull. As I went to leave, I thanked him for the money. He suddenly broke into a smile. "Don't use too much," he said, raising the fireman's hook pole high in the air.

And that was the last time I saw him.

Three years had passed. That reservoir, now under a different owner, was right there in front of us.

"Was that the last you heard of your brother?" Shino asked.

"Yes."

"What happened to him after that?"

"He died."

The words slipped out easily enough. I'd grown used to saying them ever since I was a child, after all. My sister? *She died.* My brother? *He died.* They seemed such convenient words to me. *He died.* That was all. There was nothing more to say. I didn't need to explain anything.

"Well, let's go," I said, making to leave. "It's just a reservoir, after all. We won't change anything by looking at it." But still Shino squatted there, praying quietly to the water's surface. My eye was struck by the slender white nape of her neck visible at the collar of her kimono. The sound of my footsteps echoed loudly off the water's surface, like the beating of a wooden board.

From there we went to Susaki.

Susaki was the only area in the older part of Tokyo that I had never visited; my brother had never taken me there. Once I visited him while he was living with the family of his company's president. They had been burned out of their own home and were temporarily housed in a classroom of Shino's old school. We went up to the roof together and looked out over the streets of Susaki from afar.

It was an odd-looking place. Narrow alleys were crammed on either side with garish little houses, their roofs and windows adorned with red and white undergarments that had been hung out to dry and now fluttered together in the wind. To the eyes of a country lad like me, it was a sight that aroused curiosity.

"I wouldn't mind going there," I said.

"Don't be stupid," my brother said, blushing quickly.

Susaki was a prostitutes' quarter.

As we reached the tramlines, a distant memory seemed to return to Shino. There at the side of the street, she suddenly recognized the signboard of an old shop selling *shiruko* sweet bean soup.

"Ah, I remember. Now I know where we are!"

Clapping her hands in front of her chest, she hurried on ahead of me and turned into a side road. The road sloped gently before meeting the canal, which it crossed by means of a broad stone bridge. Susaki lay on the other side of the bridge.

At the foot of the bridge on this side was a street stall. What it sold, I couldn't tell. In the shadow of a reed screen that surrounded it, a middle-aged woman with a sickly complexion, who was wearing a one-piece dress with a wide open neck, languished against the back of a bench, watching the street through half-closed eyes.

"This is Susaki Bridge," said Shino.

The stone parapet of the bridge was still marked with black

stripes where it had been licked by flames. Shino patted it affectionately with the palm of her hand. Then she looked up curiously at an arch that crossed the sky on the far side of the bridge. It bore an inscription in letters edged with light bulbs, which were presumably lit at night. "Su-sa-ki Pa-ra-dise," Shino read in a hushed voice.

"'Paradise' sounds cheap to me," she said, her cheeks flushed. Then she started off again without a word.

Shino walked briskly over the bridge. The pounding in my chest quickened of its own accord.

It was not that I'd never visited a red-light district before. Far from it—on many occasions I'd strayed into such places with friends, under the influence of drink, to gratify some cheap passing desire. But now I was about to walk these streets in broad daylight, sharing a white parasol on a sunny day with the woman who commanded my affections. This was something I could never have imagined.

After crossing the bridge, we turned into the first side alley on the left, and the red-light district was suddenly there in front of us. Its streets seemed to have withered in the sun, their color faded like that of a sick man. And the only sound to be heard in this alley, which was silent but still steeped in the seedy atmosphere of night, was the ringing of our own footsteps.

At the corner of another alley, a spot where houses of ill repute were packed together tightly, Shino suddenly stopped and turned to face me. "This is it," she said, pointing toward a shabby-looking building on the corner. "This is where I was born."

It was a firm, clear voice. Her face was tinged with self-consciousness, but there was not the slightest hint of shame in her voice.

"My mother used to operate a shooting range here. I'm the daughter of a shooting range owner from the red-light district."

Shino looked me straight in the eye and smiled, her face brimming with a kind of inner strength. That strength seemed to gather together the beads of perspiration that glistened on her brow, then sprang from her face and leapt across to my heart with a rhythm like ripples on water.

"It's all right," I said. "There's nothing wrong with that."

In my haste, I didn't even mind the way my voice sounded shrill and nervous.

Now Shino's parasol began to quiver. As she gripped the handle tightly with both hands, her fingers shone radiantly white against the deep red of her obi. She glared at me with a look of reproach.

"Look at it closely. So you won't forget," she said firmly.

I looked. I saw pink walls peeling here and there, tiled pillars rising abruptly from a cracked concrete floor, cheap Western-style balconies perched up above, and neon lights hanging over the alleyway like old cobwebs. When darkness came, this garish "house of women" would show dubiously colored lamps in its windows. But under the noonday sun, it seemed little more than a deserted building that was merely holding its breath. Here, of all places, I thought it pointless to seek the ghost of Shino's birthplace.

Something that sounded like raindrops fell on Shino's parasol and bounced back off again. Looking up, I saw a group of puffy-eyed women, their shoulders and breasts exposed, sitting along the upstairs windows of the houses that crowded around us. The women had been looking down at us in silence, resting their chins on their hands on top of the futon mattresses that were hanging halfway out the windows to be aired. Then one of the women had spat out the gum she'd been chewing, aiming it at Shino's parasol. When it hit the target, they had all snickered together.

Shino cast her eyes down and started off without a word. We walked for a while toward the heart of the area. Suddenly Shino turned to face me.

"Did that shock you?" she asked.

"Well . . ."

"I'm sorry." She apologized as if it were her fault. "I don't wish to speak ill of them, but courtesans weren't like that in the old days. When it comes to professional pride, they were in a different class then. They all seem to think it's a joke these days—it makes me nervous just to look at them. I suppose it's because times have changed, but I really can't stand these amateurish girls. I'm sure my father would be disappointed."

"What's your father like?"

"My father?" She tilted her head to one side and laughed. "He's a lazy good-for-nothing. Well, he's in poor health now, so I shouldn't be too hard on him. He was the eldest son of a dyer in Tochigi, and he should have taken over the business. But when he was young, he had little time for study, and eventually he was disinherited for it. He ran wild, threw away his education, and did nothing but drink, saying 'I'm no good, I'm a failure.' But even then, on the day of the Benten Shrine festival, he would dress up in fine clothes like *haori* half-coats made of silk. People used to call him 'Professor Atariya' in the red-light district. Atariya was the name of my mother's shooting gallery. Apparently he used to look after the less fortunate courtesans and give them advice. I remember one of them who was friendly to me, Onaka of the Tonero House. She had consumption and couldn't work anymore, but her contract still had a while to run, so she used to go to my father for advice quite often. In the end, though, there was nothing anyone could do for her, and on the Fudo Temple festival day, she killed herself by putting poison in *tokoroten* jelly and eating it. Now, the Tonero people were the most heartless lot in the whole district. They were scared, and none of them wanted to clear up the mess, so my father took care of everything from beginning to end. One evening, he loaded Onaka's coffin onto a cart through the back door. He pulled while I pushed as far as Nakanocho. Some shop clerks there happened to be using long dippers to cool the road with water from a huge rainwater tank. One by one they came and joined our cart, and helped us push it all the way to the gate of Daimon Temple. I was always doing things like that, even when I was a child."

We were now walking through Nakanocho toward that same temple gate, which I could see in the distance. We were on a broad road with a pavement, an ordinary shopping street lined with bright shops. We looked at each other and both laughed with relief at the same time.

"Haven't we walked a long way!" I said.

"Yes, but now my mind is free," Shino replied. "Now you know everything about me. I feel complete. It's a good feeling."

Shino lifted her face, closed her eyes and walked two or three steps, then suddenly stopped and took hold of my arm. We were at the foot of Susaki Daimon Bridge.

"Hey, let's go to Asakusa!"

"Asakusa? You mean, to go back to Tochigi . . . ?" The train for Tochigi left from Asakusa.

"No, just for fun. Seeing Susaki suddenly made me want to go there. My father used to love Asakusa. He often took me there. We'd see a film, then I'd ride on the merry-go-round in Hanayashiki Park, and on the way home we'd drop in to the Kamiya Bar. My father would let me have some wine while he would drink some of those very strong Denki Bran cocktails the place is known for."

"But since it's your day off, perhaps you'd better go back to Tochigi."

Shino's father still lived in Tochigi with her brother and sisters.

"Yes . . . But since it's my day off, I want to do something I can't normally do. Yes, I think I'd like to go to Asakusa."

I thought about Shino's difficult daily routine, and the excitement in her heart today. I said we should do whatever she wanted.

"Thank you!" she said and suddenly shook my arm, then caught herself and hurriedly let go again.

"But I wonder if the Kamiya Bar is still there?"

"I think it is. I have a feeling I caught sight of it once, on my way home to Tochigi. Let's see a film, then go to the Kamiya Bar. I'll have wine, and you have Denki Bran. Let's drink a toast to what I've done today."

"So I'll be your father and you'll be my daughter?"

"Forgive my disobedience, sir!"

Shino playfully ducked her head, then trotted over the Susaki Daimon Bridge, her parasol resting on her shoulder.

I'd first met Shino earlier that spring, in a Japanese restaurant called Shinobugawa, near the Yamanote railway line. I was studying at a private university in the northwest of Tokyo and was living in a student dormitory not far from the restaurant. One evening in March, I went there for the first time, after a farewell party for graduating students. Shino was a waitress at Shinobugawa.

Although Shinobugawa was known as a classic *ryotei* restaurant, it had none of the usual trappings of one, like a grandiose entrance or planted shrubs, but simply faced directly onto the metropolitan tramline. On the ground floor, it had a counter where customers could enjoy a quick drink while eating *tonkatsu* breaded pork cutlets or a variety of à la carte favorites. There was even a counter in the back where they sold cigarettes. In other words, it was like a small eating house with added frills, a modest restaurant on the outskirts of town. Few of its customers ever came by car. The regulars were schoolteachers or company employees who commuted to work from the nearby railway station, or local traders living a life of easy retirement. Occasionally they would be joined by young fish-mongers or butchers in blue suits, on the lookout for female company. The restaurant was reasonably well known in the neighborhood, and its reputation and saké prices were on the high side, so it was not the kind of place that students could go very often. My dormitory, at the end of a side street around the corner from Shinobugawa, housed some twenty students from coastal towns at the northern end of Tohoku. Many of them came from fishing families.

All of the students in the dormitory were fond of drinking. They were naturally good at holding their liquor, as if they'd been predisposed genetically to drink mugs of saké as protection from the cold. For better or for worse, and whatever else happened, drink was everything to them. They would drink in the dorm, and when that alone wasn't enough, they would go out to town. There they would toss back a few cups of strong liquor at *oden* food stalls under the railway bridges, or in bars along the tracks. Sometimes they would indulge themselves at sushi restaurants. They found it a rare pleasure to eat sushi with their drink, a treat reserved for special occasions only.

None of them ever went to Shinobugawa. They all said that they didn't like its style, or that its saké was insipid and undrink-able. But the truth was that they couldn't afford its prices. Besides, they found something unnerving about the girls who worked there. There was a rumor that one of the students, Shioda, had secretly gone out to Shinobugawa one night. He was the son of a rich fisherman, well built and handsome, and he usually had his way with girls. At Shinobugawa, he'd tried his luck with the restaurant's most popular beauty, a woman of twenty. But she'd casually brushed him aside, and he'd left crestfallen. Or so the rumor went. When they heard it, the rest of the group knew that they could never aspire to the girls of Shinobugawa.

Why did we all march into Shinobugawa en masse after the farewell party that year? Well, during the party, one of our graduating drinkers made a speech in which he looked back over his life in the dormitory. He lamented the fact that, although he'd stamped his presence on every drinking establishment worthy of the name in the entire neighborhood, he was about to return home without once setting foot in Shinobugawa. This touched off a long-harbored sense of indignation that triggered an unexpected turn of events.

That night, ten or so stalwarts trooped through the doorway of Shinobugawa, well watered with drink and strangely excited. It was a cold night, and there were no customers at the downstairs counter. We lined up in a row and called out, "Hot saké!" At that instant we all fell silent, as if our drunkenness had suddenly drained away. It was already late, and everything around us was still. Suddenly, from an upstairs room, we heard the plucking of a samisen.

"Hey! I hear a samisen," blurted out one of the graduating students. The young chef burst into laughter. That merely increased our embarrassment, and we quickly downed the saké that was poured for us.

Still, when two or three girls in kimono came to serve behind the counter, the hot saké and enlivened atmosphere restored our underlying inebriation, and we all became visibly drunk. As we did, we started spouting dialect in loud, uncouth voices, and that made the girls laugh. One student began to argue with the chef about fish, whereupon they all launched into a discourse on the subject. For when it came to fish, they could never run dry of conversation.

I was terribly drunk. I am not the son of a fisherman. Neither my drinking prowess nor my knowledge of fish could compare remotely with theirs. I rested my elbows on the edge of the counter and closed my eyes. Then the student next to me nudged me and whispered in my ear.

"Hey, look. She's the one that gave Shioda the brush-off."

Fixing my bleary eyes in the direction indicated by his chin, I saw a pair of white *tabi* socks quietly descending the stairs from the upper floor, teasing the hem of a bluish kimono as they did. The face that emerged, as its forehead parted the *noren* curtain, was that of a slightly built woman with her hair tied in a knot. Giving a sideways bow in our direction, she picked up a tray that held empty saké bottles and started along the corridor toward the kitchen. In my badly drunken state, I called her back.

"Excuse me," I said. "Could I have a glass of ice cold water?"

"Yes," answered the woman. She smiled, bowed her head with a slight bend of the knees, then disappeared down the corridor. Her feminine "yes" resonated in my ear like a haunting musical phrase.

"What? She's the one who rejected Shioda?" I muttered to myself. "I can't believe it. But you can't judge a book by its cover. You certainly can't."

With elbows propped on the counter and my chin resting heavily on my hands, I was still muttering to myself when, quite unexpectedly, I heard a woman's voice behind me. "Sorry to have kept you waiting," the voice said. I turned to see the woman in the bluish kimono, standing there with a glass. I had no idea how or when she had arrived there. Caught off guard, I gulped the water down, but suddenly felt reluctant to return the glass right away.

"You heard me talking to myself, didn't you?" I said. The woman nodded candidly, and a smile spread over her mouth with its slightly protruding lower lip.

"All I heard was 'You can't judge a book by its cover.'"

"I was talking about you," I said.

She said nothing, but opened her eyes wide.

"It was you who gave Shioda the brush-off, wasn't it?"

"Brush-off? No, it was just that he was too forward," she replied.

"So you'll only brush someone off if they're too forward?"

She giggled. "That depends on the person."

"What about me, then?" I blurted out. I suddenly felt sober.

The woman tilted her head and laughed. "Well, now. This is the first time we've met, so it's hard to tell."

"Really. All right, I'll come again tomorrow," I said without thinking.

"By all means do. Ask for me, and I'll be sure to see you right away."

"What's your name?"

"Shino."

When I awoke the next morning, I could see Shino's face float-ing in my mind's eye. I splashed my face with cold water and laughed off the previous night's drunken bravado. But when dusk fell, my mind grew strangely restless. For a while, I paced nervously around the dormitory. At length, I convinced myself that I'd made a promise after all, and should go back again that night. I would hear Shino say "yes" just once more, then leave. And I would never set foot in the place again. With that thought in mind, I furtively ducked under Shinobugawa's *noren* curtain and sat at a corner of the counter. "Saké, please. And could you call Shino," I said quietly to the serving girl.

Shino appeared immediately. "Sorry about last night," I said. In fact, the previous night's good cheer now seemed but a distant memory, and the best I could do was to drink in silence, hang-ing my head. Even then, Shino didn't seem unduly vexed, but merely watched me with a permanent smile in her eyes. Once or twice, someone came to call her from upstairs. Shino refused each time, saying, "I'm busy right now. Make some excuse, will you?"

That merely increased my discomfort. "Shino?" I said, unable to bear it any longer.

"Yes?"

My return home was more like an escape. The same process was repeated over the next ten days, but when I stopped and thought about it, I realized something strange was happening to me.

During the day, I doubted Shino. I couldn't help but feel that her friendliness was just part of her job. But when nighttime came, those doubts disappeared. I couldn't help but feel that her friendliness was completely genuine. At night my heart was full, and I'd fall asleep mocking my earlier cynicism. In the morning, however, I would awake with a sense of emptiness, despising the previous night's frivolity. As I wavered between these two emotions, I felt as though I were gradually falling into a deep, deep abyss.

One evening in June, on the spur of the moment, I told Shino that I'd last seen my brother in Fukagawa. Her eyes shone as she replied that Fukagawa was where she'd been born some twenty years previously. She said she had not been back in eight years but would like to see it again, and I casually invited her to go with me. The truth was that I wanted to have a good look at her outdoors, in the light of the sun. Shino was the customers' favorite at Shinobugawa, and couldn't easily take time off. But a month later, during her annual holiday, our plan at last came to fruition.

That was when I trusted Shino during the day for the first time.

After returning home from Fukagawa, I was overcome by a sense of shame. Shino had been so honest, and I felt ashamed that I'd been my usual cynical self. That evening, I wrote her a letter for the first time, not to beg her forgiveness, but simply because I wanted to be as honest with her as she had been with me. This is what I wrote.

There are some things I didn't mention about my family today. Now I want to tell you the truth.

I was the youngest of six children. Until I was six, I had two brothers and three sisters. In the spring when I turned seven— on my birthday, of all days—my second eldest sister killed herself. She loved a man she couldn't marry, and, in her despair, drowned herself in the sea off Tsugaru. That summer, my eldest sister also committed suicide. She was musically gifted and used to play the koto. But she was so distraught about our sister's death that she just lay her head on her koto and poisoned herself. And in the autumn, my eldest brother disappeared. He was terribly neurotic and probably couldn't bear his grief over his sisters. We still don't know where he is, so we assume he must be dead, too. My remaining brother was a capable, upright person, and we were all relying on him. He's the one who paid for me to go to university. He's the one who worked in Fukagawa. At the end of spring three years ago, he went back home, asking for money. He said he wanted to set up his own lumber company, and not only took our family's miserable fortune, but borrowed from our relatives as well. Then he ran off with the money. I have no idea why. I'm so sorry I lied to you at Kiba.

The betrayal by my brother really hit my family hard. From the shock of it, my father had a stroke. We were crushed, desperate, each filled with unbearable thoughts. These were truly dark times for us. Now I've taken over my brother's former position, and my family has once again found hope.

I've never celebrated my birthday. Somehow it feels like a day of misfortune for me and my family. On that day last year, I felt depressed and went back to Fukagawa. That was when I started walking around there. And now I always go to Fukagawa when my spirits are low. It rekindles my anger toward my brother, and I feel like a man again.

So now you know everything about me, too.

_____

I handed this letter to a sweet-natured girl called Toki who worked at the cigarette counter in Shinobugawa and asked her to pass it to Shino. The next day, Toki handed me Shino's reply, a single line written on a paper chopstick wrapper:

Let's celebrate your birthday next year.

From that moment, I belonged to Shino.

At the end of July, I learned that Shino was engaged to be married.

Shioda's family had just made a big loss in a fishing venture and had gone bankrupt. As a result, Shioda had to leave university and go back home to the country, and, as his parting shot, he let me in on the secret. For a moment I was speechless. Shino with another man? I couldn't believe it. At first I thought Shioda was merely being spiteful, as a kind of revenge for having to drop out. But he said he'd heard it from a reliable source, and he even knew the name of the fiancé—Yukifusa Motomura. What's more, he'd seen them out walking together in Asakusa.

I couldn't believe a word of it, yet my anxiety grew of its own accord, filling my mind with dark clouds of doubt. I felt as though I'd been betrayed. One day I couldn't stand it any longer and ran to Shinobugawa to discover the truth. It was in the middle of the day, and my bleary eyes were almost blinded by the sun. At the cigarette counter, Toki was taking a nap. I woke her and asked her to call Shino. Surprised at my wild appearance, Toki rushed out to the back.

Shino came trotting out, wearing only a dark-blue cotton kimono tied at the waist. She had obviously been combing her hair, which hung freely down her back. I felt as if I were seeing a different kind of beauty in Shino's appearance, a kind I hadn't witnessed before. This merely stoked my anxiety and filled my heart with despair. As I stood there in front of her, my whole body shook.

"What on earth is the matter?" she asked, knitting her brow with an expression of unease.

"You know a man called Motomura? Yukifusa Motomura?"

She drew in a sharp breath. "Who told you about him?"

"It doesn't matter. Is it true you're engaged to this man?"

Shino suddenly blinked and cast her eyes down.

"Tell me," I insisted.

"I will. I'll tell you everything. But not now, not here. Wait for me on the railway bridge at seven o'clock this evening. I'll ask the proprietress for an hour off. I promise. Please say you'll wait till then."

"At Susaki, you said you'd told me everything. Was that a lie?"

"No." She lifted her head. "I just didn't think it was worth mentioning. I would never tell a lie. I would never lie to you, even if my life depended on it."

Overpowered by the sharpness of her tone, I fell silent. We stared at one another full in the face for a few moments. I began to feel uncomfortable.

"Could you make it six, not seven?" I asked. "I can't wait until seven."

"All right. I'll be there at six. I promise."

I left Shino there with her face contorted in embarrassment, rushed out of Shinobugawa, and roamed the streets. I walked and walked, telling myself how ridiculous it all was—me, Shino, Motomura, Susaki, my letter. I stepped into a public bathhouse along the way, and scooped hot water over my body from the head down. Then, as I lounged in the massive bathtub, a thought suddenly flitted across the back of my mind. I almost said it aloud. *Take her . . .*

The blood drained from my face in an instant. Why hadn't I realized it sooner? I would take her! Even if she really *was* engaged, I would just take her from her fiancé. I swam around in the bathtub, splashing hot water to the rhythm of "Take her! Take her!" I knew I had no other choice.

I was at the railway bridge by six o'clock. Shino had arrived early and was waiting for me. Without saying a word, we walked off side by side along a deserted footpath that skirted the stone walls of the old mansion quarter.

"It happened last spring," Shino started in a quiet voice, still looking ahead. "The sales manager of a car company came and asked if I'd agree to marry one of their salesmen, a man named Motomura. The company was one of our clients, and Motomura had seen me at a New Year's party or something. He desperately wanted to marry me, so the sales manager came to ask the proprietress for permission. He said that Motomura was a successful salesman who earned a considerable income, was a good person, and had an upright character. I had just turned nineteen, and I had no idea what marriage really meant. I didn't know what to do, and, besides, I had to keep earning money to send back home, so at first I refused. But both the sales manager and the proprietress said it was a lucky break for me, and kept pressing me every day to accept. Then one day, they said that if I agreed to marry him, the sales manager and Motomura would take joint responsibility for my parents in Tochigi, as well as my brother and sisters. I was still of two minds, but eventually I gave in. What a fool I was! Anyway, Motomura was now my fiancé, and on my days off we'd go to see a film, or sit in a café, but I wasn't happy at all. I couldn't get myself to like him, however hard I tried. He, on the other hand, seemed strangely keen to hurry the wedding plans along— where we would have the ceremony, where we would fly for the honeymoon, that's all he ever talked about. It all felt somehow empty to me, and I lost interest in getting married altogether. And the more he tried to hurry things along, the more I found reasons to postpone everything. So then he . . ."

She broke off in mid-sentence and looked down at her feet as she walked along.

"He what?"

"He tried to have me."

My cheeks were flushed with indignation, and my chest pounded violently.

"And? Did he?"

"Of course not!" Shino laughed off the idea. "But he grew so persistent that I started to feel anxious, so I went to ask my father's advice. My father was so angry that sparks seemed to fly from his eyes. They'd been to Tochigi to ask him directly, but all I had sent my father was a noncommittal letter. So he had delayed his answer. He said this was a terrible way of doing things. They were forcing me into a compromising position and making me unavailable to marry anyone else. He said he'd always lived life as he pleased, and told me I should get out of a marriage that was based on conditions like that. He said I shouldn't throw my life away for such shortsighted promises. He said I should find someone I loved more than life itself and get married without a second thought."

I stopped. Shino turned to face me.

"Please break it off with him," I said.

"All right."

"Pretend it never happened. Forget about it."

"All right."

"And tell your father you've found a marriage partner who seems more to your liking."

She opened her eyes wide and looked me hard in the face. A certain heat started to swirl between us, spinning more dizzily with each new breath. We began to draw toward each other. Shino slowly raised her hands and embraced herself. I swallowed hard.

"Was that too forward?" I barely managed to ask.

"No. Not at all."

Shino barely managed to laugh.

At the end of autumn, Shino's father took a turn for the worse.

As a result of years of heavy drinking, her father had suffered from liver disease ever since the move to Tochigi, and his condition had only worsened after the death of Shino's mother. With only the money Shino sent them every month and her younger brother's income, however, he couldn't afford to recuperate properly, and with a naturally pessimistic attitude to boot he had simply let himself slide. Each time a letter arrived from Shino's brother giving detailed news of their father's condition, the bitterness was evident in Shino's face, despite her attempts to hide it. "I wish there was something I could do, but there isn't," she would say. "No matter what I do, it's never enough." And she would laugh in a desolate way. But one morning, a telegram suddenly arrived with the news that her father was dying.

Awoken by the girl who had come to tell me, I raced down the road to Shinobugawa. Shino had already made her preparations, and was waiting for me, her face ashen. "It looks like the end for my father at last. I'll be leaving soon."

With surprising composure, Shino unfolded the telegram and showed it to me. My throat felt instantly dry.

"I'll go part of the way with you," I said in agitation.

"Yes, I would like that."

"Let's leave right away."

"What, as you are?"

I was wearing a casual cotton gown with *kurume-gasuri* patterns, tied at the waist with a simple *heko-obi*. My face was unshaven.

"I suppose you'll be embarrassed."

"No. If it's all right with you."

"Well, let's go then. The sooner you get there the better."

We eventually arrived at Kitasenju, after a change of trams. Shino would take the Tobu Line from there, and would arrive at her father's side two hours later.

"What my father has is called constriction of the liver," Shino explained as we waited on the platform. "His liver keeps shrinking, and in the end it'll be the size of a pebble. There's probably no hope for him at this point."

Judging from her expression, she seemed to be expecting the worst.

"You mustn't give up," I said. If anything, I was the one who sounded more upset. "You have to be strong. And whatever happens, you mustn't let it bring you down."

As I rambled on incoherently, trying to put on a brave front, the train pulled into the station. Shino took a small folded piece of paper from her obi and thrust it into my hand.

"Please read this after the train has left."

"Send a telegram if you need me," I said. "I'll be there right away."

"Thank you."

She clasped my hands softly, then climbed into the train and set off.

When the train had disappeared from sight, I slumped down on a platform bench and opened the folded paper. It was a letter, faintly scribbled in pencil on writing paper. I turned the paper toward the light and read:

May I ask something of you?

I would like you to meet my father before he dies.

I would feel sorry for my parents if they both died without meeting you. I would be sad for myself as well.

At least I can introduce you to my father. At least he can die in the knowledge that his daughter is in good hands.

So I hope you don't mind, but would you come on the one o'clock train tomorrow? I'll send my youngest sister Tami to meet you at the station.

Also, there's something I couldn't tell you before. We live in a small Shinto shrine. When we were bombed out of Fukagawa and evacuated to Tochigi, we had nowhere to live. So we were given temporary shelter at the shrine and eventually took up residence there. I hope you won't be put off by that. Please, please come. Then I'll see you tomorrow.

I hope you can make it on time.

Or if you can't, at least come and see my dead father's face.

—Shino

I took the one o'clock train from Asakusa the following afternoon and arrived in Tochigi at just after three.

As I emerged from the tiny station building, a girl with her hair in a bob appeared from nowhere and smiled at me sweetly. With her broad nose and upslanting eyes, I instantly recognized her as Shino's youngest sister. "You're Tami, aren't you?" I said.

The girl gave a little nod and then called out my name like a teacher taking class roll call.

"How is your father now?" I asked.

"The doctor says there's no hope, but he's still alive," she said in heavy dialect, her voice rising at the end of each phrase.

"Well, that's a relief." *Shino's wish may yet come true*, I thought.

"Shino says she won't let Father die till he's seen you."

Shino must have said that to lift their spirits—after all, the doctor had given him up already. Even then, I felt myself tense at the thought that someone as powerless as I was could help to prolong, even by just a few hours, a life that was about to vanish into nothingness.

Tami led me along a narrow path that ran beside the railway track, then, turning behind the houses that lined the main road, we hurried across a field where eulalia grew in clusters. Red dragonflies flitted across a sky overcast with heavy clouds.

"Is this a shortcut?" I asked as we walked on.

"No, it's the long way around," Tami answered.

"Why are we going the long way around?"

"Well, if Father's staying alive till you get there, he might die the moment you arrive," Tami said solemnly, but when I instinctively slowed my pace, she hurried on ahead.

Near the main road ahead of us stood a little cedar forest. Crows circled the sky above it like scattered sesame seeds.

"Oh no, they're back, those crows!" Tami cried angrily.

As we approached, it turned out not to be a forest at all. It had once been a forest, but the trees were being gradually cleared from the back, leaving only a sparse wood. We passed through a decaying, crooked shrine gate and entered the wood. There, at the back of a forest of tree stumps, was the shrine building, old but larger than I'd expected, standing forlornly in front of a straw-colored field. This was Shino's family home.

As Tami raced off toward it, Shino emerged from beneath the high one-story verandah that surrounded the shrine and ran toward me in her dark-blue patterned cotton slacks, passing Tami on the way.

"Well, here I am," I said.

"Thank you! I'm glad you could make it."

She removed a towel from her head and clasped it in both hands. In the space of a single night, her eyes had become hollow, her lips cracked and dry.

"Thank goodness I made it in time."

"Yes. We've managed to keep him alive until now."

I strode purposefully toward the shrine ahead of Shino, who seemed to hesitate as she stood there biting her lip. The shrine building had none of the usual decorations, and seemed to have been out of use for some considerable time. All that remained was a single, faded cord hanging limply from the shrine bell. As I started to go in, at the place from which Shino had emerged, she called from behind to stop me.

"That's my brother's workshop. It's this way."

I climbed the shrine steps with downcast eyes.

I slid open the wooden shrine door. In the dim interior, a bare light bulb hung down like a ripe persimmon. The interior measured about twenty square yards and was divided into two halves, the rear of which was on a platform raised slightly above the floor.

There, wooden boxes and picture frames of various sizes, probably remnants from the shrine's past, lay jumbled together. The floor of the front half was covered with frayed tatami mats, and there, beneath an antique blackened chest at the back, was the deathbed of Shino's father. Beside him, Shino's younger brother, a broom-maker by profession, her fifteen-year-old sister, and her youngest sister Tami were all lined up, kneeling formally.

"Father, father! He's here, he's here!"

Shino rushed to the bedside and shook her father's chest through the thin quilt that covered him. His shriveled face was so small it was hard to believe he was an adult. The flesh had almost disappeared from his face, and bones protruded visibly under his skin. As Shino shook him, he turned his head weakly to the right and left, his eyes still closed. Shino shook him again and said my name, but he could only moan in a high-pitched voice, and he seemed to lack the strength to open his eyes.

"He's come all this way, after all . . . doesn't he understand? Do you, Father?"

Shino was on the verge of tears, and turned to her brother and sisters to seek their help. Suddenly, Tami put her mouth to her father's ear. "It's Shino's man," she said loudly. "It's Shino's man!"

He opened his eyes slightly, even before she had finished. As if to make doubly sure, the young girl continued: "Father, it's Shino's man. Look! He's right next to you!" The old man's eyes quivered as they gathered the orange light from the bulb, then crossed falteringly toward me, barely able to carry their own weight. I leaned over him and looked into those eyes.

"Father," I said.

"Ah. Glad to meet you. I'm Shino's father."

His words were slurred but his voice was surprisingly strong. He tensed his neck and tried to lift himself.

"Don't do that. You're fine as you are," I said as I pressed down on his shoulders. They felt like wooden sticks.

"I'm an old fool who couldn't even raise his own children properly . . . but you take good care of my Shino, won't you," he said, before gasping madly for breath.

"Can you see him, Father? Can you?"

Shino seemed desperate for her father to see me, and clung to him insistently.

"Yes, I see him," her father answered in a voice that was suddenly transformed, like a dying breath.

"Yes, but what do you think? What do you think, Father?"

His hollow cheeks twitched.

"He's a good man."

His eyelids drooped wearily as he continued to mouth words with no sound.

"He said he could see you. He said you're a good man."

Shino looked up at me briefly, then back down at her father.

Her tears fell softly onto the old man's withered neck.

The next day, Shino's father died.

Now Shino and her siblings had nowhere to live. Their home was returned to the shrine authority and the family had to live apart. Shino's brother moved into a broom-making company as resident craftsman, the sisters moved in with relatives, and I took care of Shino.

After fifty-seven days of mourning, Shino and I would realize her father's wish, that she should find someone she loved and get married without a second thought.

On New Year's Eve, I took Shino home on the night train from Ueno.

A fine, powdery snow was falling when we reached my home-town. As we stepped off the train and walked along the open platform, snow fell like powdered silver on Shino's hair, dressed high and held fast with gleaming lacquer.

"Hello! Hello!" my mother called when she saw us, her wrin-kled old face breaking into a smile. She held out her arms as if to hug us from afar. Unabashed, Shino went straight to my mother and greeted her with a bow. My mother bowed lower still and returned the greeting in her lilting country tone.

"Well, well, look at you, coming all this way to be snowed on!" said my mother as she brushed the snow from Shino's shoulders. Shino blushed, but sweetly let my mother finish the task.

"You needn't have come to meet us in this weather," I said.

My mother straightened her back and made a face, dismiss-ing the idea. "How could I not come to meet you, when you've brought your young lady to see us at last? Anyway, there's a taxi waiting."

We listened to the chains on the tires clank and jangle as the taxi took us along a road piled high with freshly fallen snow. We crossed a frozen river, then made a sharp right turn onto a slop-ing road that went up alongside it. It was a narrow road, only wide enough for one vehicle at a time.

"I wonder if we can get through in this snow," the driver said, tilting his head uncertainly.

"I've got my daughter-in-law in here. We've got to get through!" my mother insisted, leaning forward in her seat.

"Well! Your daughter-in-law on New Year's Day, that's grand," said the driver. "It'd be unlucky to stop halfway! Don't worry, we'll get there all right."

My father and my sister Kayo were standing by the road outside our house, huddled together under a single umbrella. The driver sounded his horn playfully, and my father waved a large wooden snow shovel that he held in his hand.

"Welcome, welcome, both of you," my father said as we stepped out of the taxi. My sister invited Shino under her umbrella with a warm embracing gesture and led her toward the front door.

"Been snowing since last night, doesn't matter how often we clear it," said my father.

"Are you sure you should be doing that?" I asked, looking up at him. He wasn't well anyway, and his back seemed more hunched than it had been before.

"Why not?" he laughed.

"He won't listen, no matter what we say," my mother said with a sigh.

Dusk came early that day. The five of us sat at a quilted *kotatsu* table in the living room, eating the little cakes we had brought as a present. My father kept asking us to repeat our story, and it was time to light the lamps before we could even finish.

As my mother and Kayo got up to make dinner, Shino stood and took an apron from her suitcase. Flustered, Mother held up a hand to stop her. "Oh, no, Shino, you're my daughter-in-law!" she said. "Just you sit down and relax."

"Please let me help you," Shino pleaded.

"It's all right, I've got Kayo to help. You just rest yourself."

Father and I laughed to see the pair arguing over an apron.

"Mother!" I called. "Shino wants to help. Can't you let her do something?"

Mother looked at me aghast. "What are you saying, son?! I'm not going to ask my daughter-in-law to work in the kitchen when she's only just arrived! What would people think?"

"It's all right, Mother. Shino isn't like other daughters-in-law. She would find it strange for a young wife not to work. Let people think what they like! You've spent your whole life worrying about appearances. Now that Shino's here, it's time to stop! Just let her help. Wouldn't you enjoy making dinner together with your newly arrived daughter-in-law?"

"Well, I suppose you're right," said my mother with a rueful smile. Shino cheerfully put on her apron, while Mother helped tie the strings behind her.

I let Shino go to bed early that night, since she hadn't been able to sleep on the train. Meanwhile, I discussed the wedding arrangements with my parents in the living room.

We decided to hold a private ceremony the following evening. Our relatives lived too far away, and there weren't many people we knew in the neighborhood. Personally, I hadn't wanted a lavish affair anyway, but I left the decision to my parents, in deference to their feelings. After all, they'd had six children, and now, at last, when they were both in their sixties, their youngest child would be the first to marry. Luckily, they agreed with me from the beginning.

My father and Kayo turned in for the night, leaving only Mother and me in the living room. For a while, we sat there quietly, the silence broken only by the hissing of the kettle on the stove.

"You've done well, son," my mother said at length. That made me happy.

"Yes," I replied simply.

"I had a good idea from your letters, but you know, until I met her, I did have my doubts. Her having worked in a restaurant and that. I even dreamed about her. But people who have been through hardship are different somehow. You'll have to treat her right, you know. Don't go taking her good nature for granted."

I nodded several times as my mother spoke. "And what does Kayo think?" I asked.

"She's happy. You'd think she were getting married herself."

I was relieved to hear that. The one thing that worried me about my marrying Shino was the effect it would have on my sister. She was in delicate health. She had been visually impaired since birth, and she always wore blue tinted glasses. This year she would be thirty-five, and she surely had no prospect of marrying now. Of six brothers and sisters, she and I were the only two left. I already felt an obligation to protect her as it was. Above all, I knew that I mustn't extinguish the little flame of hope that flickered unsteadily inside her heart. My marriage could have been a great shock for her. I was deeply concerned that Kayo, now left to fend for herself, might fall into a dangerous type of solitude—a solitude that we siblings were ill equipped to endure.

That night, I was to sleep upstairs with Kayo, while Shino would share a floor with my mother downstairs. On my way up, I peered into the kitchen to see Kayo vigorously washing her face at the sink. I knew it was her nightly routine to splash her face with cold water before going to bed, but this time, I instantly suspected that she'd been crying there until that very moment. Whatever she thought of Shino, her fragile emotions must have been in turmoil.

If I were one of our dead siblings, I would simply have gone upstairs without a word, I thought as I walked into the kitchen with intentionally heavy steps. "Hey!" I said behind my sister's back, and she turned to reveal a moistened red face. I came close to her. "What d'you think of my future wife, then?" I asked with deliberate brashness.

Kayo smiled, blinking as droplets of water trickled down over her eyes.

"She's a good person."

"She'll be like a younger sister to you! Do you think you'll get along?"

She said nothing, but smiled. Then she raised a fist, and, like a cat playfully batting at its kitten, hit me on the chest with a tenderness that only blood relations can know.

"Thank you," I said.

Now I was sure that my marriage to Shino would be a success.

The following morning the skies were clear of snow, and a full moon shone that night.

For the ceremony, I wore a kimono and *haori* half-coat with matching geometric patterns, and *hakama* pleated culottes. My parents wore formal crested garments. My father, who rarely left the house owing to ill health, hadn't worn his for more than ten years, but he'd taken them out himself from the bottom drawer of the chest, and had asked my mother to quickly iron the deep creases on the collar of his half-coat. Shino didn't have a proper full-sleeved kimono for formal occasions, and instead wore her visiting kimono, the only one she had. To keep her company, Kayo also wore her visiting kimono, fastened by a white obi with golden stitching. The five of us knelt on cushions in the middle of the guest room, a snow-covered landscape visible beyond the glass door. We occupied three sides of a square, with Shino and I in the center, my mother and father facing each other on either side, and Kayo next to my mother. Before each of us stood a miniature table bearing a large broiled sea bream.

It was a very modest ceremony, with no go-between, no *ocho-mecho* origami butterflies or other traditional decorations, no well-wishers to celebrate our wedding. There could hardly have been a smaller wedding than this, but at the same time, there could surely have been no ceremony in which hearts were more closely knit, more warmly entwined—so warmly, indeed, that we were almost moist with perspiration. And for Shino and me, there could have been no more fitting start to our married life. For our vow was that, in our own humble way, we would try to live strong, full-hearted lives.

We performed *sansan kudo*, the ritual exchange of saké cups. We had a good deal of high-class tableware in our house, remnants of our past affluence and quite unbecoming our present status. That tableware served for most gatherings, but this house had never seen a wedding before, and there wasn't a single piece that was suitable for the occasion. For our ritual exchange, then, we had to make do with ordinary saké cups. Kayo volunteered to pour, and went around filling the cups. Unfortunately, she couldn't see the saké properly on account of her poor eyesight, and consequently she overfilled the cups each time, spilling saké onto the table. "Oh no! Not again!" she would cry in embarrassment. We sat there chortling the whole time.

With the formal ceremony over, my father suddenly announced that he would sing the Takasago song, a Noh song commonly performed at weddings. His face was bright red after a single cup of saké.

We were all stunned, as we'd never heard him sing before. We made a joke of it and tried to laugh it off. But he was serious. He adjusted his pose and cleared his throat loudly. Now his right fist, which he'd placed on his knee, started to shake uncontrollably and repeatedly struck the edge of his table. He was having another attack. Ever since his first illness, his paralyzed right hand would always shake uncontrollably when he grew too excited.

"*Taakaasaagooyaa* . . ." he started, chin quivering. But he wasn't singing; his tongue was tied and his voice caught awkwardly in his throat. All that emerged was his wheezing breath, hissing out in spurts through gaps in his teeth.

"Stop it, Dad, please stop it!" my mother pleaded tearfully. But he wouldn't stop.

"Father! Father!" Kayo used both hands to hold down his shaking right arm. Yet he continued to sing, and the sound of his fist striking the table edge merely grew in volume.

I watched in silence as the three continued their struggle. To think that my parents, who had quietly endured so many betrayals by their children, could so easily lose their composure in this brief moment of joy! I thought of the happiness the three must now be experiencing for the first time, and was suddenly overcome by the urge to weep. Shino just laughed innocently, her eyes reddened with drink.

That night, Shino and I slept together in the upstairs room.

Two futon mattresses had been laid out side by side on the floor. Keeping just the pillow, I quickly folded one of them up again.

"In the snow country, we don't wear anything in bed," I said. "We sleep with nothing on. It's much warmer than wearing nightclothes."

I took off my ceremonial garments and underwear, then quickly slipped under the quilt completely naked.

Shino took some time to fold her kimono. Then she switched off the light and came to kneel by my pillow.

"Am I not allowed to wear nightclothes, then?" she asked timidly.

"Certainly not," I answered. "You belong to the snow country now."

She said nothing. I heard the rustling of cloth in the darkness, then a moment later, "Excuse me" as a dim white shadow slipped in beside me.

That night, I made love to Shino for the first time.

Her body was fuller than I'd expected. Usually, she only wore a kimono and tended to look on the slender side. Yet her breast was larger than my palm when I took it in my hand. Her flesh was firm, but felt as though it would yield indefinitely if I pressed it. Her skin was delicate, and when we brought our bodies together I could feel the pulsing of her blood beneath it. Every crevice in her body was hot, as if burning from inside. Our bodies were instantly moistened with sweat.

That night, Shino was a perfectly fashioned puppet, and I was an inexperienced puppeteer, forgetting himself at his first performance.

We lay awake, still locked in a close embrace.

"What do you think? Warm, isn't it?" I said.

"Yes, very," she replied, her mouth at my chest. "Let's sleep like this always, even when we're in Tokyo."

Shino then recalled our wedding ceremony and said how much she liked my family. "I'm ashamed at my uselessness," she added. "I'll try hard to learn from now on. Now that I'm here with you, I realize that I've wasted these twenty years of my life. Always putting myself last, never saying what I do or don't want, and all for the sake of others . . ."

"That's the Shino of Shinobugawa."

"Well, I'm going to forget all about Shinobugawa now. Starting tomorrow, I'll be a new Shino. From now on, I'm only going to think about us. Let's be sure to have a good life together."

As her voice trailed off, the deep snowbound night felt as still as the grave. Yet from the very edge of that stillness, we could hear the sound of jingling bells, growing louder as it approached.

"What's that noise?"

"It's a horse sleigh."

"What's that?"

"A sleigh pulled by a horse, of course. One of the local farmers has probably been up to town, had too much to drink, and has only just now gotten back home."

"Can I see?"

Still naked, we wrapped our bodies as best we could into one large quilted kimono and crept out of the room together. When I slid open the shutter on the landing window, a shaft of light as cold as a blade painted Shino's naked body a harsh shade of white.

A horse sleigh moved along the snowy mountain road, pulling its dark shadow behind it. The snow shone as bright as day. The driver was slumped asleep on the sleigh, huddled in a blanket. The horse raced along as if hurrying home alone, its shoes gleaming brightly in the moonlight. As we stood captivated by the scene, Shino gave a little shiver.

"Let's go back now," I said. "We'll be on the train again tomorrow. We ought to get some sleep."

"All right. Let's fall asleep before the bells fade away."

We hurried back to the warmth of our quilt. Shino pressed her frozen body against my chest and quietly placed her chattering teeth against my shoulder.

The sound of the bells gradually faded into the distance, until all I could hear was a ringing in my ears.

"Can you still hear them?" I asked.

But Shino didn't answer. I placed my lips against hers. She was already asleep.

The next morning, we set off on our honeymoon.

We hadn't originally planned to do anything half so formal, but my mother insisted we should go, even if just for one night. Not only for our own sake, but because my family had to make various preparations for their lives from now on, too. So it was that, with some reluctance, we decided to go to a hot-spring resort two stations to the north of my hometown, for one night only.

The resort was in a village nestled in a mountain gorge, where I'd passed a lonely year in those dark, dreadful days when I was forced to quit university. I wanted to immerse Shino's body in the cloudy white waters of the hot spring there, waters in which I had once washed away the sweat of my turbulent mind. For it was that same turbulence that had culminated in our meeting in the first place.

The morning train was packed with itinerant traders going about their New Year business, but we were lucky to be able to sit facing each other. Shino narrowed her eyes, swollen from lack of sleep, and gazed out at a landscape bathed in morning sunlight.

Not long after we'd left the station, Shino gasped and opened her eyes wide.

"I can see it! I can see it!"

She suddenly grabbed my knee with both hands and shook it.

"Look! I can see it, I can see it!" she repeated, pointing out of the window.

Outside lay a town of squat houses with snow piled high on their roofs, accompanied by ice-bound rivers, bridges, lookout towers, temple roofs, and the low, flowing profile of the Kitakami mountains in the distance beyond.

"What? What can you see?"

"My home! I can see my home!"

Looking carefully, I could just make it out, there by the craggy edge of the frozen river: my parents' house, its white walls tinged with the color of the morning sun, making it stand out from the snowy whiteness.

"Oh, yes. I can see it."

"You can see it, can't you! My home!"

Shino shook my knee harder still. In all her twenty years, she had never actually lived in a proper house. It wasn't hard for me to understand the joy she felt at glimpsing her newfound home, in the distance, from the window of a train on the way to her honeymoon.

I suddenly noticed that the other passengers—traders carrying the first wares of the New Year, others dressed up for their first visits of the year—had fallen silent and were staring at us curiously. I nodded to Shino in silent affirmation, while in embarrassment my face turned a shade of crimson.

Shame in the Blood

WHILE I WAS STILL at university, I married Shino, a young woman of twenty, who worked in a *ryotei* restaurant near my student dormitory. We married during the New Year's holiday, less than two years after we first met.

During my winter vacation that year, I took Shino back to my hometown, where we held a modest wedding ceremony witnessed only by my family on the evening of January the second. The next day, at my mother's insistence, we set off for a brief honeymoon in a rustic hot-spring resort nearby.

The road to the resort was barely wide enough for a single horse to pass through; beyond that was a snowy landscape that stretched on endlessly. Our inn had a large sunken hearth in the middle of its reception area, and thick white spa water welled up in its hot-spring bath. Apart from that, there was nothing remarkable about the place at all. Of course, I felt ashamed at the plainness of it, but Shino seemed happy enough. "I've never seen so much snow!" she declared cheerfully. "It's the perfect place to celebrate our marriage." Standing at the window, she surveyed the winter scenery and the hazy flurries of snow in the distance, then, turning back to the decorative alcove in our room, laughed when she noticed that our *mikan* orange had rolled off its two-tiered rice cake again. The orange had fallen off repeatedly since the morning. There was no draft in the room; it just rolled off by itself. Each time it fell, Shino would pick it up and put it back on the rice cake. Then a few minutes later, off it would roll again. And so it went on.

"They're both frozen solid!" said Shino. "That's why the orange keeps rolling off. What do you think we should do?"

"Why not leave it as it is?"

"It's a New Year's decoration! We can't do that!"

Shino thought for a moment, then put the frozen orange under our quilted *kotatsu* table to thaw it out.

That evening, we took a bath in the hot-spring water. There was something I needed to tell Shino before we turned in for the night, but try as I might, I hadn't found the right moment to say it during the day. Though I knew it was not the kind of thing you should tell your new bride on your honeymoon, it was a matter I simply couldn't avoid. At the same time, I realized that it could cast a shadow over Shino's cheerful mood.

I sat on the edge of the wooden bathtub, listening to the wind race over the fields outside. Every now and again, the bathroom window would suddenly mist over. However tightly we shut the window, wispy snowflakes would somehow find their way in and flutter down onto my warm back. They brought me back to my senses and gave me renewed courage.

"You know, last night I made sure you wouldn't get pregnant," I said.

It took Shino a while to follow my meaning.

"Oh!"

She blinked and looked down.

"Do you want to have children?" I asked bluntly, just to make sure. Shino crossed her arms over her chest, blinking hard, as if she was unsure exactly what I was asking.

"Well . . . of course."

"How many?"

"Two. A boy and a girl . . . but it doesn't have to be right away."

"Really?"

I sighed and looked out of the window. It was just as I had thought.

Shino said nothing for a while.

"Why?" she asked eventually, as if something had been left unsaid.

"Well, actually, I don't," I said resolutely. I watched Shino's expression. As I'd feared, her face betrayed disappointment. Even so, she managed to force a smile.

"Why? Don't you like children?"

"No. It's not that."

"Well, is it because you're still at university?"

That wasn't the reason either. I was already a student husband.

If I had wanted children, there would be nothing to stop me from being a student father as well.

"So, is it because I'm not good enough, then?" she said with an unusually self-deprecating smile.

"Don't be silly," I replied. Shino was the wife I wanted. I obviously wasn't going to pass her over to have children with someone else.

"All right, if you're going to start saying things like that, I'd better be plain. The truth is, I'm scared of having children," I said.

Shino nodded and looked down at her feet, as if the truth had finally come home to her. Perhaps she had imagined this moment when she'd agreed to marry me.

"You know why I'm scared?"

"Yes."

I was relieved not to have to repeat the whole wretched story again.

My parents had six children, myself being the last. Of those six, none of the first five were normal. Two committed suicide. Two disappeared. And two were handicapped from birth. One of them even suffered two of these misfortunes. Four were already dead or missing. That left only myself and my sister Kayo, whose vision had been severely impaired from birth. As the last remaining brother, I couldn't help feeling deeply troubled about their tragically short lives. I couldn't believe that their individual fates were merely an unrelated series of accidents; I felt sure they were all strongly tied together by some invisible thread. That would explain why they all slipped so easily into decline after the first suicide.

Imagine a couple that has a handicapped child. No doubt the couple feels sad about their unexpected misfortune. But what would happen if they then had a second handicapped child? Would they simply continue to be sad? Or imagine a family in which someone commits suicide. The survivors may well feel more anger than grief. But then, just as they're all saying what a senseless act it was, another member of the family does exactly the same thing. Could they simply remain indignant? The shock that would hit them then would surely surpass all feelings of sadness or indignation. They would surely feel that there must be some fatal connection between their unfortunate family members.

To me, it all came down to blood. My suspicion was that the very blood that linked us all could itself be tainted. And the most frightening thing was the inevitable reality that the tainted blood of my siblings also ran through my own veins. I would have to live my whole life fighting the deadly lure of my tainted blood. I felt a terrible self-loathing when I realized that my life would be a constant struggle against my own blood. So it was only natural that I should feel a terrible fear of passing this blood on to my children—blood that could cause my own ruin at any time.

I had already told Shino of my family circumstances several times, but she'd agreed to marry me in full awareness of them. When I said I was scared of having children, she didn't laugh. She must have known very well that this fear of mine was no ordinary anxiety of a young father-to-be. But now she had heard her own husband declare unequivocally that he preferred not to have children. How did that make her feel? Thinking about it was really more than I could bear. Shino, though young and healthy, was to be denied what was probably the greatest joy that a woman could know. Of course, she herself had chosen this unhappy path, but it was I who had pressed that choice upon her. The realization of that caused me great heartache. For a while, we sat there listening to the sound of the wind, each lost for words to say. I started to feel a chill.

"Aren't you cold?" I asked at length. "Let's warm ourselves in the bath." I stepped into the bathtub, beckoning Shino in after me. We entwined our fingers tightly under the steaming, milk-white water of the hot spring.

"Of course, I know how you feel," I said. "But I'm just not confident enough right now. Otherwise I would do it here and now. So will you promise not to ask for a child until I'm ready?"

Shino nodded and tensed her fingers.

"It's all right," she said. "Don't worry on my account. I'll wait until you're ready. After all, there are couples who can't have children, aren't there . . ."

"So that's a promise?"

"Yes."

Shino loosened her fingers and moved her body away from mine.

After our one-night honeymoon, we stayed with my parents for another ten days. Then, when my winter vacation was over, I returned to Tokyo alone.

On my way to and from university each day, I would walk past the restaurant where Shino used to work. Sometimes the young girl who had worked with Shino would part the *noren* curtain and come running out.

"How are things, then?" she would ask precociously.

"What things?" I would ask in reply.

"Shino, of course! Is she all right?"

"Oh, yes, she's fine. She's been throwing herself into her housework, you know."

"Any little ones yet?"

"Don't be daft!"

Occasionally the proprietress would come out, her gold teeth gleaming.

"Shino's living with her mother-in-law? I wonder how she's managing."

"Oh, she seems to be managing all right. Breaking ice to fetch up water, learning her needlework, that kind of thing."

"Really. Well, I'm glad to hear it. But you know, it must be hard living apart when you're only just married."

She seemed to cast a look of concern at me as she said that.

We had decided to live apart until I could graduate from university. I still had just over a year left, and the ordeal of my graduation thesis still awaited me. I knew I would be unable to concentrate on my studies if Shino were by my side. I was too weak-willed. I feared that if we lived together I would simply become too preoccupied with her and manage no work at all. Shino, for her part, wanted to become better acquainted with my family, and in the process, she could brush up on the household chores that she had not had occasion to practice for so many years.

Though we lived hundreds of miles apart, it didn't seem so terrible to me, perhaps because we had never lived together anyway. In any case, it wasn't such a bad thing for us to live apart most of the time, then meet in an intense way every now and again. About twice a week, I would write Shino a letter in the style of a diary entry, and about once a week Shino would reply with news of my family. Then, as soon as my vacation started, I would shoot back home like an arrow. Shino would come to meet me at the station. On our way back to the house, she would take a calendar from her obi and throw it into the river from the bridge. She used to make those calendars herself. She would count down the days until I was home again, crossing off each day as it passed. When the last day on the calendar was crossed off, she knew I would be home the next day.

We spent the spring vacation together, then the summer. Soon it was November.

One evening, an express letter from my father arrived at my apartment in Setagaya. I had moved there from the dormitory to complete my thesis. My father had always been calm and placid by nature, and ever since he'd had a mild stroke some years earlier, even the smallest thing had become too much for him. He would rarely send a letter, let alone by express mail. I hurriedly opened the envelope, thinking perhaps that my mother was ill. But it wasn't my mother. It was Shino—she was having morning sickness.

The letter was written in my father's faltering hand:

*I know this might interrupt your studies, son, but there's some-
thing I think you ought to know. We were having dinner about a
fortnight ago when Shino suddenly felt sick while she was eating
a green pepper. As you know, she loves green peppers. But ever
since then, she's been sick whenever she smells them. Not just
green peppers, but any food with a strong smell. Your mother
said she'd seen Shino secretly spitting something out in the sink
before that, and had guessed what the cause of it was. Since then,
Shino has been violently sick every day. These days she can't even
take rice soup. A week ago, your mother took Shino to the hospital and asked if they could examine her. The doctor asked about
Shino's condition. He asked how many days it was since you
went to Tokyo. Then he did a calculation on a piece of paper, and
said this could be a matter for the maternity ward. So then they
went straight to maternity and asked for an examination there.
The doctor said there was a strong chance of good news, but that
we'd have to wait another week before he could know for sure.
Having fathered six children myself, I know a bit about these
things. One evening, I went out to the shops to buy some* mikan
*oranges. Without saying anything, I put them by Shino's pillow
that night. When I looked again about an hour later, they were
all gone! Today is the seventh day since they went to the hospital.
Shino has been for another examination, and it turns out she's
expecting after all. They say she's already two months along.
This being your first experience, I thought it might be a bit of a
shock for you, so I wanted to keep it under my hat till you came
back at the New Year. But this is a big milestone in your life, and*

*a uniquely happy event for our whole family, so I couldn't keep
it to myself even for one day. Now, you're not to worry about
Shino at all. She is thinner, but now we know that her sickness is
natural, I'm sure she'll soon have her chubby cheeks back. On no
account are you to go all womanly on us.*

There was a postscript:

*You know, when I think I'm to be blessed with my first grand-
child after all these years, I reckon it was worth getting old after
all! I was just having a laugh with your mother about that.*

I sat in stunned confusion.

Never had a letter from my father been so brimming with
confidence and joy. Those past betrayals by my siblings must
surely have crushed his spirit, robbed him of his vitality and
made him inwardly ashamed at being their father, but now he
could suddenly write "having fathered six children myself" as
if he was proud of it. He hardly ever went shopping for anything, but now he had gone "out to the shops to buy some *mikan*
oranges" as if in triumph. The mere fact that his youngest son's
wife was pregnant was "a uniquely happy event," so much so
that a man who was usually unable to joke about anything could
now quip that his young daughter-in-law would "soon have her
chubby cheeks back." I could feel my father's unforeseen delight

coursing through each line of his letter, pulsing with a rhythm of excitement. As for the subject of the letter, I just couldn't believe it. Even if it was beyond doubt that Shino was pregnant, how on earth had it happened when she was always so meticulously careful? Perhaps she had unwittingly broken our agreement, or perhaps intentionally so, in her unbearable longing to have a child. Perhaps this. Perhaps that. In the end, unthinkable thoughts flitted through my mind, thoughts that were an affront to Shino's honor. My mind was all at sea.

Whatever the case, I knew I had to see her as soon as possible. One thing was certain: the vow we made on the night of our honeymoon had already been broken. I wanted to see this miraculous pregnancy of Shino's for myself—not in a "womanly" way, as my father had said, but with a manly resolve. This was no time to be worrying about my graduation thesis.

The next day, I left in haste for my little hometown near the northern end of Honshu.

When I arrived, Shino was sleeping alone upstairs. I opened the sliding door with deliberate roughness, calling "Hey! I'm home!"

Tears welled up in Shino's eyes as soon as she saw me. She took her hands from under the bedding and stretched them out to me as if seeking my help. When I clasped them in mine, she pulled me toward her with uncanny strength, then wrapped her arms around my neck and clung to me in helpless desperation.

"I'm sorry! I'm sorry!" she repeated in a timorous voice, mixing her words with sobs as a child would do.

Without knowing why, I felt intuitively that, whatever had happened, Shino hadn't deliberately set out to do it. She wasn't responsible for it at all. At the same time, I realized how powerless she must have felt every day in her present state. I understood her anxiety at the changes taking place inside her, changes that not even she could comprehend.

"It's all right. Don't worry yourself now," I said, removing her arms from my neck and gently resting her head back on the pillow. I gazed at her face. How she had changed!

Perhaps it was her hair. She had gathered it into two plaits, which hung down behind her ears. This must have been how she looked as a child. But her complexion was too poor to be that of a child. Her eyes were sunken and the flesh of her cheeks was hollow. Shino was like a little girl who had succumbed to some mysterious illness and could no longer summon the will to resist.

"Father sent an express letter. It was such a shock. I had to see you. I know most of the details from the letter. But how could it have happened? We were both so careful!"

"I still don't really understand. But while I was lying here, I thought back carefully, and suddenly I did remember one occasion . . ."

"When?"

"The day you went back to Tokyo at the end of the summer . . ."

I almost cried out. Yes, I remembered. It was the evening of my return to Tokyo at the end of August. I felt the blood rush to my cheeks.

It was about two hours before I was due to leave. I was getting changed upstairs. Shino, wearing a navy cotton kimono, was kneeling beside me and packing my things into my suitcase. When she'd finished, she snapped the fasteners shut, then let her shoulders sag as she remained kneeling there.

"What a long time," she said with a sigh. "September, October, November, December. Four months. Four times thirty, that's a hundred and twenty days . . . what a long time. This will be the longest, won't it."

"I suppose so. But for me it's better that way. I have to finish my thesis before the end of the year."

I said that to distract my mind from my longing for her. As I was putting my socks on, I noticed a penholder lying on the floor, by the leg of my writing desk.

"Here. You've forgotten something," I said, picking it up.

When I turned toward her, I noticed the shape of her back as she knelt there. My eyes were captivated by the unexpected sensuousness of that sight. Shino turned her head without a word, and gazed at me over her shoulder. The tint of her eyes at that moment somehow stirred my desire for her. I suddenly felt as though I were perspiring, and playfully poked Shino's cheek with the penholder. But it had the opposite effect—that of drawing me closer toward her. I quickly put my arm around her neck and pulled her down onto the floor.

It was an impetuous moment spurred by the pain of parting. It was all too hurried, and ended inconclusively. I knew that Shino could very well have conceived on that day, but since it was blatantly clear, to both Shino and me, that it had finished inconclusively, I gave it no further thought. Looking back, what difference did it make what we thought? Our bodies clearly had other ideas altogether.

"It's terrible. We're not even allowed a moment's indiscretion," I said. A bitter feeling of regret started to engulf me.

"I know. I could hardly believe it myself. But the doctor said it must have been about August the thirtieth or thirty-first. August the thirtieth was the day you left. That was the occasion I'd remembered. I was so embarrassed."

Shino's pallid cheeks took on a rosy flush, as if her embarrassment had returned. But this was no time to cling to feelings of shame or regret. The knowledge that the fetus in Shino's womb was alive as we spoke, and, what's more, was growing with every passing second, urged me on.

"Anyway, we can't change it now, can we. What about the baby? What do you want to do?"

"Me? I'd rather not have it." Shino looked me straight in the eye and spoke with startling clarity.

I felt oddly disappointed. "If that's what you want, it's probably the best. You seem awfully sure about it."

"Well, you know, ever since this happened, I've done nothing but think about it. After all, we made a promise, didn't we? And to be honest, I don't want to have a child that's been conceived by accident. I would only feel sorry for it. When I have a child, it must be something that I want more than anything. I must be glad to have it. Not something that just happens through carelessness. I don't think I could go through with it just because there's no alternative. Does that sound strange?"

"No, it's not strange. You're right. I'm behind you on that."

"Really? Well, I'm glad to hear that. At least we know we can have children whenever we want. And we can learn from our mistakes."

Shino smiled. Her face was a picture of relief.

That night, I talked it over with my parents. A few days later, Shino had an abortion at the hospital.

The following March, I closed the book on my student days and went back home for a while, then, in June, returned to Tokyo with Shino. We embarked on our new life together, in the apartment that I'd used as a student.

A full year and a half after we were married, we could at last live alone together. But from the outset, our new life was beset with hardships. The problem was that I had no job. In my final year at university, I had taken a test with a view to joining a newspaper company. Before the test started, I was asked to complete a detailed questionnaire about my family, yet found myself unable to write a single honest word about the lives of my brothers and sisters. So I walked out without completing the test, and from that time on lost all desire to look for work. Never before had I felt so resentful about the ghosts of my dead siblings, which seemed to haunt me wherever I went. Never before had I so wanted to reject a society that seemed more interested in those ghosts than in my own personality. For the first time, I truly longed for a world that would accept me for my own work, regardless of the ghosts I carried on my back. My "work," I decided, would be to write the stories of each of my brothers and sisters, and I immersed myself in that while living a life of quiet seclusion with Shino. In the real world, of course, such a life was impossible to maintain. We were hounded daily by the grim specter of poverty.

A year passed.

The following summer found us in the very depths of penury. I received a telegram from home saying that my father was seriously ill. We promptly went back to the country, taking nothing but the clothes on our backs. My father had a disease called encephalomalacia—softening of the brain. We nursed him for seven days and seven nights without sleep, witnessing in minute detail the sight of a human being dying a natural death. And on the morning of the seventh day, my father died just as normal people did.

My father's plain, ordinary death left a profound impression on me. I'd grown accustomed to abnormality in my blood relatives, after all. For me, it was a kind of salvation. The feeling of inferiority that I'd always harbored about my kin suddenly dissipated, and I felt a strange brightness before my eyes. It may sound callous, but I couldn't help feeling touched by joy rather than sorrow. I was seized by the urge to tell everyone that, yes, my father had died an ordinary death.

That very same day, I went to the hospital and told the doctor who had treated him. "My father passed away this morning," I said. "Thank you for everything you've done."

I went to the local temple and told the head priest. "My father died a natural death this morning. I hope you'll take care of the funeral."

I greeted these people with a cheerfulness that even I found embarrassing.

After my father's death, only my sixty-eight-year-old mother, my thirty-eight-year-old unmarried sister, my wife Shino, and I remained.

At the wake, my mother knelt in a small huddle in front of me. "Son," she said, "you're the only one we can turn to now. Don't let us down. If you went off like the others, who would look after Kayo, Shino, and me? We'd all die in misery, for sure. You're the only one we can turn to now. Please, for mercy's sake, don't go copying your brothers and sisters. I beg you, son."

She bowed low, revealing a tiny bald spot on the crown of her head, a remnant from the days when she used to tie her hair in a topknot. Then she stood and tottered off to the funeral feast.

I focused my mind on the path I would now tread as "the survivor." It was no longer a path I would tread alone, nor just with Shino. For I had three companions now. If I were to lose my footing and slip off the path, I would pull the other three down with me. I was no longer free to indulge myself. My brothers and sisters, on the other hand, had been free to do as they pleased. They'd given me contemptuous looks and muttered, "It's all right, there's always *him*. He'll look after everything," before falling away as they saw fit. But when their last remaining brother looked around, there was nothing left behind him. Nothing but three women clinging to his waist, looking up expectantly . . . at me. Out-of-work, impoverished me.

Now was the time to rid myself of their ghosts once and for all. I was standing on the side of the living. I had no freedom to do as I pleased, no choice but to keep on living. To maintain relations with those brothers and sisters no longer held any meaning for me. In fact, we'd never really been proper siblings. Only when they looked at me contemptuously, planning to leave the responsibility to me—only then, perhaps, were we truly related. Apart from that moment, they had done nothing but haunt me with their ghosts and their tainted blood. True, I shared that tainted blood with them, but I felt that if I could rid myself of them and mingle with the living, my blood would become healthy; it would become the blood of the living.

That thought gave me renewed strength. It flowed, from nowhere in particular, into every corner of my being. I wanted to use that strength to start something meaningful, both to mark my separation from the ghosts of my siblings and to prove myself a reliable companion for my living relatives. But at first I couldn't imagine what a person as powerless as myself could achieve.

Then, on the day after the funeral, I was clearing the drawers in my father's desk when I came across a slip of paper bearing a list of boys' and girls' names, about ten of each. I showed it to my mother and asked if it was all right to throw it away. She looked up at me and smiled sadly.

"That's from the time when you were a student and Shino was pregnant," she said. "Don't you remember Dad's letter? He said that when his grandchild was born it would be his job to think of a name. He thought and thought, but those were all he could come up with. You won't be needing them, will you. Yes, throw it away."

I felt a lump in my throat, and gazed at the list of names without actually reading them.

It was at that moment that I first wanted to have a child. To mark my separation from the ghosts of my siblings, from their tainted blood, I would borrow some of Shino's vitality and create a new bloodline. Useless and poor as I was, that was the one solitary thing I could do for my aging mother.

I went around to the back of the house, looking for Shino. She was squatting beside the well and washing clothes. As I stood there behind her, my knees seemed about to give way.

"Shino?" I said.

"Yes?" she replied, turning toward me.

"It's time."

"Time for what?"

"Time we had a child."

She seemed to gasp. Her eyes widened.

"I'll tell you about it later. It just came to me suddenly."

"Are you serious?"

"Of course! Would I joke about such a thing?"

Seeing my smile, Shino quickly turned back to the washtub and started scrubbing the clothes with renewed vigor. Her back heaved and shook as streams of soapy water flew far and wide, even reaching the dahlias that bloomed beyond the water drain.

I carefully calculated Shino's monthly cycle and chose a night that seemed most auspicious.

In a way, it would be our first night. The first real night that we would spend together naturally as man and wife, with the full intention of starting a family. We restrained ourselves and waited for that first night.

Eventually, that night arrived.

For a fleeting moment, I prayed for our child.

And from that day on, we passed our lives in relaxed contentment, as if we had fulfilled an important task. All we could do was to wait for a sign that Shino was pregnant. I was sure that she had conceived. Not as some kind of hunch, but as a firm conviction. I didn't know why I felt such certainty. It seemed quite irrational to have such faith in the capricious workings of the human body, especially as it was only our first attempt, but I simply had no doubt that our labors on that night would bear fruit.

For the same reason, I now kept myself apart from Shino at night. I was worried that my longing to relive the pleasure of that night would unwittingly extinguish the flame of new life in Shino's womb. To protect that possibly nonexistent flame, I was afraid to enter Shino's body simply for the sake of lust.

Shino continued to work breezily and energetically as before. She would apply herself to any task with fervor, and appeared to exude a sense of fulfillment. A vibrant life force emanated from within and her face showed not a hint of the sorrow that sometimes clouded her appearance.

Seeing Shino in this light, I imagined that she was being energized by a maternal self-awareness. It seemed proof enough that she shared my conviction. But occasionally she would come and sit quietly by my desk, as if plagued with doubt. Perhaps it was only natural, since it was she who would carry this pregnancy. She would sometimes wear a pensive expression and appear to be listening to the sound of her womb.

"Everything's going to be fine," I would say. "Just believe it and wait."

"Yes, but it's all right for you," she would reply with a smile. "I have a heavy responsibility. I can't be so casual about it." She would thrust her chin out at me as she said the last part, then stand up and shuffle off again in her slippers.

About two weeks later, the first change came over Shino. She had a discharge of blood ten days before her period was due. She announced it to me with a look of dismay on her face; she felt that she couldn't be pregnant if she was discharging blood. She thought it must be an irregular period, and said that a similar thing had happened before without any warning. But I, unacquainted with the workings of the female body, for that very reason had every confidence in the ten-day slip. To me, a sudden slip of ten days in a regular cycle could not merely be explained as an "irregularity."

Two weeks after that, we drove up to the highlands to see the autumn colors, taking some of my sister's koto pupils. On the way home, Shino was sick at the smell of gasoline.

That decided it: she was expecting. Now she had to tell my mother about it. Erring on the side of caution, however, she wanted to have it confirmed by a doctor first. So one day we went out to the local clinic, on the pretext of taking a walk.

The clinic was near the river. I decided to wait on a long bridge that stood halfway there from our house.

"See you later, then," Shino said as she started off from the bridge. "Don't be angry if we're wrong."

"I won't be angry. Don't worry."

Shino walked off, clasping the ends of her thin shawl together in front of her. From the end of the bridge, she took a narrow path down to the riverbank, then followed the river around the foot of Inariyama, a hill topped by a Shinto shrine. Once she had disappeared from sight, I started pacing up and down the bridge, smoking incessantly. When a cigarette seemed about to scorch my finger, I would hurriedly shake my hand and send the butt flying into the river. Strange insects would follow it down like jet planes. This scene was repeated over and over again.

A long time I waited there.

Eventually, I heard a woman's voice calling "Hey!" from the sky above me. I looked up and was surprised to see Shino standing among the withered bushes halfway up Inariyama. She must have taken the shortcut over the hill from the clinic on the other side. Not only did the shortcut involve a steep climb, but the ground was also strewn with tree roots. *What an idiotic route*, I thought.

"Hey!" Shino called again.

"How did it go?" I shouted back.

"We've done it!" she answered, raising her arms in a triumphant salute.

"Told you so," I called. I could feel a smile coming over my face. Taken by the urge to shout at the top of my voice, I called again:

"Boy or girl?"

For a moment, Shino looked puzzled. Then she put her hands to her mouth and leaned forward to answer.

"How should I know!"

She started to run down the hill. Startled, I wanted to shout out a warning, but found myself entranced at the sight of this woman as she made her way down the hill, her shawl fluttering from her neck, sleeves swaying wildly to right and left, and the hem of her kimono flapping violently as she ran. She ran like a woman who'd never worn a kimono in her life.

Don't run like that! What would happen if you fell? I thought, as I braced myself nervously in the middle of the bridge.

Homecoming

AS A NEW DAY dawned in early spring, I found myself looking out through the window of a northbound train, gazing at the rural landscape as it flitted by. Outside, a vast plain stretched out under a gloomy leaden sky, its distant edge covered in low-hanging clouds.

Every now and then, the bleakness of the plain was broken by scattered remnants of snow that gathered up the meager light of dawn as they drifted past. At the corner of that bleak vision, I could just make out the dim, pale shape of my wife's down-turned face.

Shino was asleep in the seat opposite me, her drooping head swaying with the movement of the train as her arms hugged her swollen belly of seven months. She had fallen asleep as we'd pulled out of Ueno Station the previous evening, and had slept through the night without once waking. Now, perhaps, her labored mind could finally relax, released from the strain of daily life. We were at the edge of the Sendai Plain. Soon the land would start to rise and swell, and by the time Shino awoke at last, the plain would be surrounded by mountains—the Kitakami to the right and the Ou to the left. We were traveling back to my hometown at the northern end of the long Kitakami valley.

It was the third time we'd made this journey together.

The first time was three years earlier, when we went home to get married. I was still a student at the time, and Shino had been working in a small Japanese restaurant. On that first occasion, neither of us could get any sleep, given the novelty of the situation and the barely controllable excitement in our hearts. All night long we spoke in surreptitious whispers or stole furtive laughs about anything and everything that came to mind. What we found to talk and laugh about, I can no longer remember.

The second time was about a year after I'd graduated from university and we had begun our married life in a Tokyo apartment. It was in the summer of the previous year. I had received a telegram saying that my father was seriously ill, and we rushed home with nothing but the clothes on our backs. We were in the depths of poverty at the time, and had saved no money for such contingencies. It took time to scrape the fare together, and it was a full twenty-four hours after the telegram came that we arrived home. In our distress at the delay, neither of us was able to sleep on the train. Shino prayed that my father's life would be prolonged, while I, for my part, convinced that we would be too late anyway, was irritated the entire time.

And now, as we made this third journey home, poverty had finally broken us. We had abandoned our life in Tokyo to return to the country. Shino, physically exhausted and heavy with child, continued to sleep soundly—so much so that I grew concerned for her well-being. In contrast, I couldn't even doze. I was tormented by a sense of defeat, a lingering sense of attachment to the life we had left behind. Even if Shino awoke, we would have nothing to talk about anyway. We could only gaze at the rural landscape as it flitted by.

What have I actually achieved in these last two years?
Frankly, nothing at all!

Sometimes, I would close my eyes and repeat this exchange inside my head, expecting to tire of the monotony, so that I might just fall asleep naturally. But as my ears grew accustomed to the rhythm of the train, I started to hear, interspersed with that rhythm, an indistinct sound like fallen leaves being blown along by the wind. Shifting, scraping, shifting, scraping. That made it quite impossible for me to sleep.

It was the sound of an empty ice-cream carton, completely dried out on the steam heater and moving back and forth with the rhythm of the train. Shino had complained of a dry throat, and I'd emptied my pockets to buy the ice cream just before our departure from Ueno the previous evening.

Shino had eaten half the ice cream in no time at all before passing it to me with an apology. I had taken a little slurp and handed it back to her. With another apology, she'd finished off the rest, then gently placed the little round carton on top of the steam heater.

Shino couldn't bring herself to toss the empty carton under her seat, as most other travelers would have done. It was certainly not out of some crass hankering for more; I knew that the object of her attention was not the ice cream, but the empty carton itself. Her sense of caring for such a trivial thing may have been pitiful, but it was certainly not crass. For that reason, though the sound prevented me from sleeping, I was loath to remove the carton altogether.

Still the sound continued, shifting, scraping, shifting, scraping.

It had a pitch that only I could hear, and spoke to me continuously. As it did, the image of that ice cream carton stood out starkly in my dull mind. It slowly started to come apart, as if dissolving in water. The base of the carton came away from the conical body, and was now just a circular piece of cardstock. The conical body split along a vertical line, and was now a flat, trapezoidal piece of cardstock. The circular piece and the trapezoidal piece lay side by side, and, as I watched, started to multiply. Hundreds, thousands of pieces were piled on top of each other in an instant, and soon formed two tall towers. When the towers had reached a certain height, they started to bend, then collapsed with a thunderous roar and scattered to every corner of my mind.

For a moment, Shino stood transfixed, gazing down at the mass of paper cardstock that now lay scattered on the floor.

A shriveled, empty wrapping cloth hung limply from her hand.

"I'm home," she had said, sliding open the screen that divided our tiny hallway from our tiny room. With the full cloth bundle still in her hand, she had placed one foot on the threshold, then, with an "Oop-lah!," had lifted her swollen belly over it, whereupon the knot of the cloth-wrapped bundle had suddenly unraveled.

At length Shino gave a deep sigh. "Aah. If only they were biscuits," she said as if to herself.

Shino was twenty-four and had been married for more than three years. It was comical, in a sense, that a woman of her age and status should speak so childishly, but I could find no reason at all to laugh at her. For she had almost forgotten the luxury of eating sweets. In her typical way, as if embarrassed by her own wishful thinking, Shino tilted her head, gave a little giggle, and started to gather up the pieces of cardstock that lay scattered over the floor. She placed them in separate piles, one for the round bases, another for the trapezoidal sides. But there were hundreds of each type, and they were all mixed up together. It would have taken her forever to pick up and sort them all on her own.

"Excuse me," she exclaimed, overwhelmed at last, "do you think you could give me a hand, if you're free?"

I was sitting at my desk in a corner of the room, wearing a quilted kimono.

"In olden days," I said sternly, "if a lady was with child, the lord of the house would scatter beans all over the Great Hall, and would make the lady pick them up again. From a standing position, you understand. She would stoop to pick them all up, one by one. Now, you might think this was dangerous, because it would put too much pressure on the woman's belly. But in fact, each time she stooped, she tensed her belly, thereby making her stomach muscles stronger. What's more, the exercise prevented the baby from growing too big, and that made the childbirth smoother. Where I come from, they make pregnant women swab the floors of wooden corridors morning and night. Exercise is important in pregnancy. It would be good for you now and again, don't you think?"

"So you're a lord now? Well, well! A lord in a padded dressing gown!"

"Aha! The dressing gown is merely the outward appearance of one who lives *incognito*," I said, standing at last. "You gather the bases and I'll pick up the sides."

These two types of card were the materials for making ice cream cartons. Twice a week, Shino would collect them from a man who lived in an alley full of antiquated houses, about ten minutes on foot from our apartment, and would bring them home wrapped in a large cloth. She had set a small table by the window, where she would busily assemble the cartons.

It was a side job that Shino had started about a year earlier. "Perhaps I should get some work," she had said quite unexpectedly, lifting her face from the POSITIONS VACANT section of the newspaper one day. The meager savings we had when we married had just run out, and poverty suddenly stared us in the face.

"Work? What sort of work?"

"Well, I wouldn't be sure about working in a bar or a coffee shop. But a restaurant would be all right. I'd have no problem with that."

Shino seemed confident that she could use the experience from her old job.

"Don't be silly," I said, cutting her short. "Otherwise, what was the point of leaving your last job to get married? You shouldn't waste your time on idle thoughts like that."

"But I feel so useless just hanging around here doing nothing."

"It doesn't matter. You're all right here. I couldn't bear it if you started running around all over the place. If we're ever that desperate, I have some ideas of my own. You don't need to worry yourself."

Actually, I didn't have any specific ideas to revive our flagging fortunes. In fact, no sooner had I uttered those words of empty consolation than our financial straits started to worsen by the day.

About ten days later, Shino came home in high spirits.

"Good news!" she called as she opened the front door. "I've found a job that I can do at home. I saw it on a poster, on a telegraph pole in front of the market. I wonder why I didn't notice it sooner. Isn't that good news? Say you'll let me do it!"

The job involved assembling ice cream cartons.

"Forget it," I said.

"But why? It's well paid, and I can do it at home whenever I like. They'll come and collect when I've finished. And I'll make sure I don't disturb you. Please let me do it!"

She then explained how she had followed the map on the poster to a house at the end of an alley, and had already agreed to do the work.

I never thought for a moment that Shino's side job could earn us enough to live on. The very idea would have been a psychological burden for me, and I thought her foolish for not realizing that.

I couldn't even bring myself to laugh at her folly when she told me about it. But we were paupers, after all. What choice did we have? Our only other prospect was to resign ourselves to our poverty. In that case, perhaps it was better to be engaged by something, to immerse ourselves in it and thereby to endure the worst.

"All right, then," I said. "You'd better give it a try. But just to tide us over, you understand."

"Of course. That was my intention. I'll stop as soon as you tell me to."

The next day, Shino went straight over to fetch the materials. Between our tiny room and our window was a narrow wooden-floored area, neither a verandah nor a corridor. She placed a small table under the window and busily started assembling the cartons there.

Every three days, her employer from the end of the alley, a bearded, middle-aged man, would come to collect the finished cartons. He would ride up with a large box tied to the rack of his bicycle, which he would pull up under our window. Then he would tap on the window with his finger, and call out my wife's name in a gentle voice that belied his appearance. If the sliding door between our room and the wooden-floored area was open, Shino would hurriedly close it. Then she would open the window, and place the cartons, piled together in tubes, into the box on his bicycle rack, counting "One, two, three . . ." as she did. When she'd finished, the man would ride off again, calling out "What a lovely day!" when it was sunny, or "We certainly need this rain!" when it was wet. Then he would go around four or five other houses collecting cartons in exactly the same way.

Shino started the work in early spring. As summer approached, the man started coming every other day, sometimes every day. As always, he would tap on the window with his finger and call, "Hello there! How is it going?"

"I'm sorry," Shino would reply, "I haven't finished yet. It's not going badly, but I've too many other things to do."

"Really? I'm running out of cartons, you see, so I need some urgently. How many do you have left to do?"

"Oh, about seventy or eighty, I think."

"Well, could you just let me have what you've finished so far?"

"Really? All right, will these do?"

"Yes, that will be fine."

As I listened to their exchange from behind the sliding door, it sounded to me like a dialogue between a popular writer and his editor.

"You're popular," I said to Shino after the man had left, half in irony, half in jest.

"It seems so," Shino replied ingenuously. "It does make my fingers hurt."

She turned back to the little table, and busily started assembling cartons again.

Soon Shino's earnings from this work would be our only source of income. At best, we could have used the money to pay our rent, with hardly anything left over. Luckily, our landlord allowed the rent to fall into arrears, and so we were able to eke out a living in this way. The landlord, a likeable man and a plasterer by trade, was also from Tohoku. "Ah well, money comes and goes," he had said. "We're all hard up sometimes. Pay it when you can."

The more Shino's work prospered, the more unstable my mind became. It wasn't so bad when I was feeling confident in myself, but when I was feeling insecure, it made me utterly miserable. When attaching the base to an ice cream carton, Shino would first lay the base piece on a shaping block, then place the conical piece over it and pat it down with her palm. The sound of her patting used to cut me to the quick. Shino would pile the finished cartons into long tubes and stand them in a corner of the room, making the tubes look like gigantic pencils. On one such occasion, I had a vision that this forest of pencils was rebuking me for my laziness, deriding me as useless, and forcing me to work harder. "Stop that patting noise!" I wanted to shout. But if Shino had stopped, we would have lost our only source of income. My mind was buzzing with irritation. It was too much to bear, and I rushed outside.

Our apartment stood beside a concrete canal that flowed through the outskirts of the Yamanote district. I walked behind the houses, along the edge of the canal, over a bridge and up a narrow path through a thicket of bamboo grass, to the top of a hill where some army barracks once stood. From there, I could survey the whole area around our apartment. I could see our window. I squatted on the stump of a cherry tree at the edge of the hill, and slowly smoked a cigarette as I looked down toward our window.

It was in the spring before my final year at university that I had moved into the apartment. Until then I'd lived in a student dormitory, but I came to this area to find a quieter room where I could finish my graduation thesis. I visited a friend who lived in the neighborhood, and he took me to see a real estate agent whom he knew. After listening to my requirements, the agent said he had the perfect place for me, and with that led us to the plasterer's house by the canal.

At the time, the plasterer's house was only a small, single-storey building. Apart from the family quarters, all it had was the little room he was proposing to let. The room had a tiny hall-way on one side and a window on the other. When you opened the window, you could see the canal and, beyond that, the hill covered in a thicket of bamboo grass.

More than anything, I liked the tranquility of the place, and decided to rent the apartment at once. But when I handed him the cash deposit, the landlord said he would like to see my name card. Being just a poor student, I obviously had nothing of the sort. So the real estate agent tore a page from his notebook, and told me to write my personal details on it in lieu of a name card. First I wrote my home address in Aomori Prefecture. "You're from up north, are you? Well, you can always trust people from up north," he said beside me, evidently trying to reassure the landlord.

Next I wrote that I was attending Waseda University. The agent turned to the landlord. "Be thankful he's not at Hosei," he said. "They're all lawyers there. They'll try to find holes in the contract and cause nothing but trouble."

Finally, when I wrote that I was studying French literature, the real estate agent looked positively jubilant. "Oh, look! Buddhist literature," he said. I could only think he was deliberately mis-reading the Chinese character for *French*, which is also used to write the word *Buddhist*. He said, "You'll be a priest when you go back up north, will you? As I thought—a very serious-minded young man." He must have thought Buddhism sounded more serious than French.

And that was how I came to live in the apartment. I had already married Shino at the beginning of that year, but thought it better to live apart until I could finish my thesis. I covered the window with a green curtain that Shino had made, and lived there alone for a year. Once, after a friend had come to visit, I walked him back to the nearby Tamagawa tramline stop, and on my way home, took the route over the hill. Even from the top, I noticed how vividly green the curtain looked. Just like that cur-tain, I myself felt a sense of freshness then. I was burning with hope; though poor, I was full of energy.

And now? I couldn't even tell where our window was with-out straining my eyes—and it wasn't because there were more windows than there had been before. After finishing university, I had gone back to the country for a while, returning with Shino some months later. In the meantime, the plasterer's house had changed to a grand two-storey building with plastered walls, enclosing our apartment completely on one side. No, that wasn't the reason. The curtain itself had become faded and dull, and was now the color of decomposing grass. To make matters worse, it was stained with various shapes here and there, formed by the wind and rain that blew in through crevices in the window. The curtain was now so flimsy that, if tugged on with even a slight force, it would surely rip and tear. And now, just like that curtain, I myself had become shabby and poor.

I had graduated from university, yet still had no job. I sat at my desk writing every day, but the stories I wrote showed no prospect of earning any income at all. Even so, I had no desire simply to leave my desk and go looking for jobs, aided by newspaper advertisements or the like. I never lost sight of the hope that the story I was now writing might bring success, and this was what kept me tied to my desk. If this story were to fail, sheer disappointment would drive me on to the next one. If the next story failed, I would stubbornly start all over again.

I was like a mule being pulled along by an invisible rope. Perhaps I was being pulled to the slaughterhouse. I certainly couldn't say where I was heading, but still I clip-clopped along. I didn't feel like stopping, nor pulling back on the rope. After all, even a mule has his pride.

Our humble surroundings must have seemed positively palatial to Shino's brother and sisters in Tochigi, for they came to visit us in turns. Having lost both their parents, they probably regarded us as substitutes. Shino's younger brother and two younger sisters looked up to me as an "elder brother," which was the title I'd gained by marrying their elder sister. But as the youngest of six siblings myself, and, what's more, quite distant from the other five in age, I'd grown up without knowing what it meant to have siblings. While it was highly amusing to be seen as an "elder brother," I felt a new and unfamiliar joy in relating to them as siblings. Whenever they came visiting, the inside of our feature-less apartment was as if suddenly flooded with a bright, cheerful light.

Shino's brother Kaname was twenty-one and a broom-maker by profession. He was a simple, honest young man—almost annoyingly so. He always wore the same loose-fitting, sky-blue suit on his visits and, with the earnest face of a pupil question-ing his teacher, would quiz me on bizarre trivia that had long puzzled him. "Can you really die if you eat tobacco?" he would ask, or "Do goblins really exist?"

Once he produced a pale pink envelope. "I got this letter," he said with a grin. "What should I do?" I opened it. It contained the lyrics of a popular song about first love, with numbers writ-ten alongside the verses. And at the bottom: "This song expresses my feelings for you. From Aiko."

The older of the two sisters, Sayoko, had finished junior high school three years earlier, and now did household chores for their relatives in Tochigi while helping out with her brother's broom-making. She had a boundlessly cheerful nature, and a sonorous voice—in fact, it would be fairer to say that she pro-claimed rather than spoke. "I'll never marry" was her catch-phrase. She was a hard worker whose single ambition was to save up until she could have her own shop selling *shiruko* sweet bean soup.

The youngest sister, Tami, was in her sixth year at primary school. She was shy by nature, and whenever she spoke to some-one, she had a nervous habit of patting the other person with her fingers. This must have been calming for her, since when she was unable to do it, she would become tongue-tied. Her favorite foods were potato croquettes and rice cakes filled with bean jam.

Kaname usually came alone, but Sayoko would always bring Tami in tow. They would stay for a day or two and then leave, having stirred up the stale air of our apartment. During their stays, I would always ask the same question as evening approached.

"Kaname (or Sayoko, or Tami)? What would you like for dinner tonight? Don't be shy. Say what you really want."

My pompous attitude was not out of some secret desire to flaunt my authority as the "elder brother." It was because I wanted to make the evening meal a cheerful occasion, if nothing else. Their sister had left them in their tender years to come and live with me, and when I saw her siblings sitting right there before me, I couldn't escape a sense of guilt that I'd stolen her from them. Of course, I would never have presumed to make amends merely with a single dinner. But it was the best I could do, every now and again, under my present circumstances.

After taking their requests, I would work out how much money was needed and select a few tomes from my bookcase. "I'm just going out for a walk," I would say. "I won't be long. Let's all go off to the bathhouse later."

Then I would exchange glances with Shino and make my exit. Once outside, I would hurry along to the local shopping center.

One of the shops was a secondhand bookstore called Kunugi Shobo. I always went there when I had books to sell. The owner, a young man with a high forehead and handsome features, was usually upstairs, while downstairs at the counter sat a slender woman with arched eyebrows; she was evidently his wife. Whenever I took books there to sell, the woman would push aside the *noren* curtain and call upstairs. Then the stairs would creak as the man made his way down. This being a regular event, I always felt rather embarrassed to see him, but when he saw me he would nod in recognition and seem even more embarrassed.

From the first time I went there to sell books, I imagined with virtual certainty that he too, like me, was a mule being pulled along by an invisible rope. I never saw him sitting at his desk, but I had a very strong sense that we were kindred spirits. I was sure he had a desk in his upstairs room, where from dawn to dusk he would sit and write short stories, just as I did. When his wife called him, he would put down his pen and rise from his chair. This imagination quickly became a firm conviction when, one day, I saw ink stains on the fingers of his right hand as he made his way down the stairs.

In fact, he must have known everything about me before I knew anything about him, not only from our unspoken sense of kinship, but also from the type of books I took there. My books were well out of fashion and had little chance of finding a buyer, but he always bought them at absurdly high prices, perhaps through the goodwill of a like-minded book-lover.

The prices he paid were half as much again as what the other shops offered. As I accepted the money, I felt gratitude and sympathy in equal measure.

"Well, thank you," I would say.

"Thank you very much," he would reply.

After a simple exchange of greetings, I would leave the shop.

Sometimes I felt we had grown so familiar that I wanted to sit and have a heart-to-heart with him, but then I thought that this might disturb his studies. Besides, it almost seemed wrong for two proud mules like us to actually introduce ourselves. And so I would always leave without further ado.

In this way, the gaps in my bookcase gradually widened until, by around the summer of the second year, only a few volumes remained. I would soon have to sell those, too, to stop the pain of Shino's toothache.

On my way to the Kunugi bookstore for the last time, I thought that I would let the owner set the prices, so as not to put undue pressure on him. Then I would say, "Actually, these are the last I have. Thank you for buying them all, you've really helped us a lot. Now I would like to ask you a favor, if I may. Would you place my books as far back in the shop as possible? I hope to be able to buy them back in the near future, you see."

Letting him know that I hoped to buy the books back seemed the best way to reward him, nonchalantly, for his nonchalant goodwill.

When I reached the shop, the glass door was closed, and so too the curtain behind it. A sign announced that the shop was closed today. In my disappointment, I was already planning my return the following day, but Shino's toothache had grown so bad that she'd been unable to sleep for two or three nights. She was already beyond the limit of her endurance. Though regretting that I couldn't make my final sale to Kunugi, I reluctantly went to another shop and sold the books cheaply before returning home.

The contents of Shino's dresser, part of her wedding dowry, were also gradually emptied, little by little. By the time the bookcase was completely empty, the dresser, too, was totally weightless. Just stepping on the floor near the dresser made it shake violently, the handles all rattling in unison.

It was I who had persuaded Shino to sell her things, but it was her job to take them to the shop. She had volunteered herself for the role, in the hope of softening up the pawnbroker. Shino owned a number of kimonos, a legacy from her former profession. She took each one individually, wrapped neatly in a *furoshiki* cloth. As she arrived at the pawnbroker's, she would stop abruptly, sniff the antique smell that emanated from the cloth bundle, and only then step into the shop, pushing the *noren* curtain aside with her forehead.

Finally, when we had literally nothing left, the telegram telling me of my father's illness arrived from my hometown. We somehow scraped together enough money to go back, but at the time it was as much as we could manage to plan for the journey home, and thinking of the return to Tokyo was quite out of the question. My father died, and we stayed in my family home for a hundred days. We had no particularly pressing affairs in Tokyo, and besides, my old mother and sister were too upset for us to consider leaving any sooner.

Shino conceived while we were there. This was no accident of her monthly cycle, but something we had actually planned. It may have seemed ill-advised to deliberately plan such a development when our lives were already so impoverished, but I had always been one to attempt things that seemed ill-advised or ill-timed, and to start a new chapter of my life that way. One example was my "student wedding." Another was my life of unemployed poverty in Tokyo. And now I was planning to have a child. Whether it succeeded or not was of secondary importance; first, I had to do it. Then I would experience the fullness of life as I went along. That was my only possible way of living. If I couldn't live like that, I felt I would never escape the miserable fate that had been etched onto my bloodline.

For the return fare to Tokyo, my mother gave me half of Father's condolence money, monetary gifts received from the funeral guests. I waited until Shino's morning sickness had eased, then, at the end of November, we set off once more for Tokyo.

Two days after we returned to Tokyo, we went on a rare outing to the local shopping center. Whenever we had any money, we were seized by the irrational urge to spend it quickly, perhaps because we had grown so accustomed to living in poverty. Of all the many things we wanted, we enjoyed wavering over which to buy first. The cash we'd brought back from the country had nearly all gone toward repaying the money we'd scraped together to travel home. But we still had a little left for ourselves.

We decided to spend the remainder on presents for each other, each buying something we thought the other needed most. Since the money ultimately came from the same purse, we weren't obliged to mimic such bourgeois habits, as if we both had separate means. But being so poor made it harder to choose for ourselves the one thing we wanted more than anything.

I bought Shino a wool scarf. Chill winds would soon be blowing, and the back of her neck looked awfully cold with no winter coat and her hair tied up.

Shino gave me a pair of *geta* wooden sandals with base supports. My old ones were so worn down that you could hardly tell whether they were elevated at all. If I stepped on a pebble on the road, they would bend like plywood.

At the *geta* shop, Shino let me choose the ones I wanted. I chose a sturdy-looking pair lined with bamboo. After paying for them, Shino asked if I wanted to wear them straight away.

"I might as well," I answered. "With these old ones, it's like walking on thin ice. They make my toes cramp."

Shino turned away from me and discreetly spat on the soles of the new sandals, then turned back and handed them to me.

"There you are," she said.

What a strange thing to do, I thought, as I slipped on my new sandals and walked out of the shop.

"Why did you spit on them?" I asked outside.

"It's a magic spell!" she replied theatrically, then looked down and giggled.

"What sort of spell?"

"To keep you from having affairs!"

She blushed as she continued to laugh.

"My, women have a difficult time of it, don't they?" I said with a wry smile. "Even with a husband in my state, you still can't feel secure. What woman would look twice at a pauper like me?"

"Not all women are after money, you know," she replied, quickening her pace.

"Really."

"There are some who don't care about that kind of thing. They're the ones I'm afraid of."

She quickened her pace again.

We continued in this vein until we arrived in front of the Kunugi bookstore. Or so I thought—it must have been an illusion, for there was no Kunugi bookstore. Perhaps it was a little further on. I looked around uneasily as we continued to the end of the shops, but the Kunugi bookstore was nowhere to be seen. We retraced our steps and returned to the place where I first thought it had been. It was now a dress shop called Charme.

"That's funny—I'm sure it was here. I'll just go and ask." I don't know whether I said that to Shino or to myself, but soon I was pushing open the spanking new door of the dress shop as I made my way in.

"Excuse me?" I called. "I hope you don't mind my asking, but wasn't this once a bookshop called Kunugi?"

At the back of the shop, a woman dressed in black was standing with arms folded and staring at a naked mannequin. She turned to look at me.

"Yes," she said, "so I hear."

"So did the owners move to another address?"

"Well, I don't really know much about it," she said. She was wearing furry house slippers and seemed to be measuring out the shop floor in paces as she slowly walked toward me, her arms still folded. "But I did hear that they closed the shop and went back to the country."

"What? Back to the country?" I inadvertently raised my voice in surprise.

"Ah, you've come to collect money, have you?" asked the woman, misinterpreting my meaning. "Well, you're not the first by any means. It seems they more or less disappeared overnight. I've sent all the others around to the landlord. If you want his address . . ."

"No, that's fine. Thank you."

I made a perfunctory bow and hurried out.

"What did she say?" Shino asked.

"She says they've closed the shop and gone home," I answered.

"Gone home? Where?"

"To the country, of course."

As I said that, I felt an icy gust blow through me. Shino looked up and stared at me wide-eyed for a moment, then blinked and looked away again.

"Perhaps business was slow," she continued.

"I guess so. Surely it's not because they paid too much for my books?"

"Surely not . . ."

Surely it wasn't. But that didn't stop the anguish I felt inside.

The Kunugi couple must have been driven out of Tokyo by debt. I couldn't help feeling personally involved. I remembered the young husband with his intelligent face—my "kindred spirit"—and his slim wife with her arched eyebrows. They had a respectable shop and worked hard as a couple, but were still driven back to the country. In that case, what cruel failures lay in wait for us? We had no shop to offer hope of a modest income, and we were totally dependent on Shino's paltry side job. Yet she was in the latter stages of pregnancy, and in any case, her income from assembling ice-cream cartons had fallen markedly now that winter was upon us. When I thought about these things, the wintry streets felt colder still.

The fate of the Kunugi bookstore cast a shadow over our future.

One day toward the end of the year, Shino's sister Sayoko paid us an unannounced visit. She wore a short red coat and sandals, and came empty-handed.

"You're on your own?" asked Shino. "Where's Tami?"

"I'm on my own!" she said with a giggle, then knelt and bowed low before me. "Welcome back to Tokyo! Not long until the New Year now!"

It was a singularly inappropriate greeting for a girl of eighteen to give her seniors. I instinctively looked over at Shino, but she just stood there looking down at her sister grimly.

"Yes, we're back now. Thanks for your help while we've been away," I joked, hoping to laugh off the curious greeting.

"No problem," she replied. "Money sure is tight in Tokyo, isn't it!" She knitted her brow in a grown-up way, probably as a reply to my joke. Her manner was no longer that of a teenage girl.

"Sayo!" Shino called sternly. She seemed to feel that something was amiss and could no longer hold back.

"What?"

"You're working in Tokyo, aren't you?"

Sayoko shrugged her shoulders and poked her tongue out in jest.

"Correct!"

"Where?"

"A place called Uncle Katsu's. In Ikebukuro."

"Uncle what?"

"Uncle Katsu's, I said! It's a *tonkatsu* restaurant," she said with a smile.

"Just as I thought . . ." Shino slumped down on the tatami floor. She was lost for words, and looked up at me for help.

"Why a *tonkatsu* restaurant, of all places?" I asked obligingly. I was equally astonished, but laughed as if it was nothing.

"Well . . ." Sayoko grinned back as she began to explain.

One day in September, a neighbor of hers in Tochigi, a middle-aged woman, had told her it was a waste for someone who'd graduated from high school to be helping out at a broom-maker's. She had asked if Sayoko would like to go and work in Tokyo. Since the woman seemed to be a good person, Sayoko had said that she would, as long as her brother and younger sister didn't mind. When she'd asked Kaname, he had said, "Do as you please, I'll be in Tokyo myself before long." Tami had said, "Yes, if you promise I can go on the school trip." Sayoko had promised, and had let the woman take her to Tokyo. "Well, all I ever wanted was a proper job. I'd been itching to do that," she finished. With that, she punched the air with her fists, like one of our wartime gym training routines.

"What's it like then, this Uncle Katsu's?" I asked.

"It's just a little restaurant. The owner's thirty-seven. He wears a hat like this"—she raised both hands above her head to depict a chef's hat—"tilted to one side. And why does he wear it tilted to one side?" she asked. I had no idea why. "Because he's got a bald spot above his ear," she continued, covering her mouth with her hand as she convulsed with laughter. "It's so funny! His wife's thirty-six. She's a bit loud sometimes, but she's not bad. They've got two children. The older one is a girl, and the little one's a boy. And that's about it."

"Hmm," I groaned, overpowered by Sayoko's quickfire speech.

Shino had listened in silence until this point, but now joined the fray. "What about the customers? What sort of people are they?"

"Well . . ." Sayoko held out her hand as she counted on her fingers. "There's a bartender . . . a street musician . . . a cabaret manager—he brings a different woman every day. Students . . . hoodlums . . . and some others. I don't know what all of them do."

Shino reacted nervously. "Now wait a minute, Sayoko," she said. "Getting a job doesn't mean you have to work in a place like that!"

"Why not?" asked her sister, looking up at Shino in utter bemusement. "What's wrong with a *tonkatsu* restaurant? You used to work in a restaurant, didn't you? I can't see how there's much difference."

Shino blinked and cast her eyes down. "Yes, but in Shinobu-gawa we didn't have customers like that. Ours were university teachers, respectable shop owners, section managers . . ."

"And students, no? After all, hubby was a student then, wasn't he? He came to see us the day before Father died, didn't he, wearing his student uniform? Looking like this?" Sayoko placed both fists on her knees and lowered her head shyly, in imitation of me.

"Don't you be so cheeky!" Shino scolded. Her cheeks started to redden.

"Well, anyway," I said soberly, "I may well have been a student. But you know, Sayoko, we're not saying one restaurant is good because its customers are university professors, and another is bad because it attracts street musicians. What we are saying is that you're still young, and your environment is important, wherever you work. If you must work, surely it would be better to work in a bright, safe environment than a dark, dangerous one. What your sister means is that she doesn't mind you working, but that you should be careful about what environment you choose."

Sayoko nodded quietly.

"That's just what the schoolteacher said."

"Leave that job, Sayoko," said Shino.

Her sister made a sullen face. "What, and go back to Tochigi?"

"Preferably, yes. But if you really must work here, I'll help you find something better."

"Well, that'd be all right, but I'm not going back to Tochigi."

"Why not? You could help your brother a bit longer. Making brooms is a decent occupation, you know."

Sayoko looked puzzled. "What? Didn't he tell you?" she said, breaking into thick Tochigi dialect in her evident surprise.

"Tell me what?"

"He's not making brooms anymore. He works in a bicycle shop now."

"What?!" Shino threw back her head and exchanged glances with me. "What on earth for?"

"How should I know? Why don't you ask him yourself?"

Shino glared at her silently before closing her eyes and breathing a long sigh.

That evening, Sayoko taught us the secret of making perfect *tonkatsu* breaded pork cutlets. When she'd left, Shino and I had a serious discussion about her family, beginning with Sayoko. We agreed that we should persuade her to leave Uncle Katsu's. But since the restaurant would be at its busiest during the New Year period, we thought it would be unreasonable to make her quit right away. Instead, we decided to inform the restaurant's owner of our intentions, then have her leave the job completely on the tenth of January. In the meantime, we would look for a better environment for her. As for Kaname's change of occupation, there was no point in doing anything without first talking to him in person and hearing what he had to say.

"Anyway," I said. "Let's invite your brother and sisters here for New Year's Eve. We can celebrate the holidays together. Then we'll discuss what they plan to do from now on. There's something I want to tell them as well. Let's do that."

"My stupid brother and sisters . . . I'm so ashamed of them," Shino said with downcast eyes. "And it'll be too expensive to feed them all . . ."

"That doesn't matter. This isn't like other New Years. Your family could break up altogether if we don't act now . . . It's time to pull out the big guns."

"You mean . . .?"

Shino frowned and turned toward the built-in closet. "The big guns" referred to my best suit, which Shino had packed away at the back of a wicker trunk. If someone were to show an interest in my literary efforts, I could wear that suit and meet them without too much embarrassment. If we pawned the suit, on the other hand, the five of them could spend two or three days that felt almost like a real New Year to them. Of course, I hadn't abandoned my work altogether. But it was fairly obvious that I wouldn't be needing that suit in the foreseeable future.

Late into the night, Shino wrote an express letter to her brother Kaname, while I wrote to the daughter of a distant relative from my hometown who also lived in Tokyo. She worked in a nylon sock factory along the same tramline that we used. I inquired whether her employers were hiring any factory girls.

Suddenly we heard a voice shouting loudly from the vicinity of the canal. "Merry Christmas! Merry Christmas!" It was the plasterer, our landlord, his speech slurred. He was obviously drunk.

"What? Is it Christmas today?" I asked.

"No," Shino replied. "Tomorrow is Christmas Eve."

"Ha! The clown's so drunk he doesn't know what day it is."

"Oh, but look. It's past midnight. So strictly speaking, it is Christmas Eve already."

As we spoke, the voice began yelling something else. We listened again.

"How about that, then! My little boy was born on December twenty-fifth! Just like Jesus Christ! How's about that, then! Merry Christmas!"

Shino and I looked at each other and snorted with laughter.

Kaname and Tami arrived from Tochigi on the afternoon of New Year's Eve.

"Sorry, this is all I could manage," said Kaname, passing me a long-handled broom wrapped in newspaper. I removed the paper to reveal a work of great craftsmanship, its straw bristles carefully sewn at the top with green thread.

"Thank you," I said. "This is the first time I've seen your work. It's really beautiful."

"Well, it's one of the best I've made," he said with an air of pride.

Sayoko came running in to join us as evening fell, and our modest home took on an unusually festive atmosphere. At dinner, I drank a small bottle of cheap warmed saké. When I was a student, I could drink saké by the barrel, but I'd recently become so weak that I already felt pleasantly intoxicated with just a single, small bottle.

"By the way, Kaname," I started, choosing my moment carefully. "Sayoko tells us you've left the broom-making business?"

Kaname glared at Sayoko. "That's right," he said with an uneasy laugh.

"And you're working in a bicycle shop now? So why did you give up making brooms?"

"Because they're all made by machine now. The handmade

ones are outdated. In two or three years they'll all be machine-made, I should think. We just can't keep up with the volume, see. Yes, I should think handmade brooms are finished now."

"Really," I said. It seemed a good enough reason. "So what about the bicycle shop?"

"Oh, well, the owner of the local bike shop asked me to join him if I was free, so I went there for a while. I'm not there now, though."

"Where are you, then?"

"Hitachi."

"Hitachi? You mean the Hitachi factory?"

"That's right. I'm a lathe operator."

Taken aback by the speed of his career shifts, I simply stared at him for a moment. Then I pulled myself together.

"Now," I started, "I'm going to say this because I think it's better said before the old year's out. There's something I'd like to ask of you all. Of course, I don't mind you going out to work. But before you do, I'd like you to come and ask my advice first. I'd just like you to come to me, and talk your ideas over. Since I'm living here with your sister, and since there's nothing else I can do for you all, I'd like the chance to advise you, at least. How about it?"

To be frank, I envied their freedom to change jobs as they pleased, and even as I spoke, I was inwardly enjoying my first attempt at behaving like an older brother. But they all sat in silence with downturned faces, as if they'd mistaken my offer for a reprimand.

"Hey, I'm not angry!" I said with a patronizing laugh. "If you've got an opinion, say it out straight. Let's talk openly."

Kaname quietly lifted his face.

"The problem is, how could we come to you for advice? You wouldn't understand our situation. It stands to reason. Someone who doesn't work can't give advice like that. We wouldn't really feel like coming to you for advice unless you were working too."

As he spoke, his face betrayed no sign of contempt, no hint of hostility, no smile of derision. His eyes alone shone brightly, as if some exceptionally luminous body were housed within them. He was only honestly stating his feelings with his usual expression and his usual voice. I was mortified, nonetheless, by his complete calm.

"So it's all right to go changing jobs all the time, is it?" I said. If anyone, it was I who sounded hostile.

"People like you who've graduated from university, you can stay at home all day without working," Kaname continued in the same even tone. "But people like us can't make a living unless we work every day. We haven't got time to pick and choose our work. The jobs won't wait forever, after all. I like working. I'll try my hand at anything. And when I find the thing I like best, I can carry on doing it all my life, can't I? That and nothing else."

Having said his piece, Kaname gave a little shrug.

What hurt most of all was the realization that, in the minds of Kaname and his sisters, we lived in completely different worlds—they as "working people," I as "someone who doesn't work." That was how perverse my unproductive life appeared in their eyes. I now knew that, related as we were, I could never be in the same circle as them, and that made me feel unbearably desolate.

"All right, but at least you could write to let us know when you change your job or your address. Otherwise we won't know who's doing what and who's living where. That could be a problem if something happened."

Far from enjoying my performance as the older brother, I was now imploring them.

Writing letters was not their strong point. They looked at each other and shrugged.

Soon after New Year, we had a favorable reply from the daughter of my distant relative. She said that four or five of her colleagues would be leaving the factory in mid-January, and that she might be able to recommend Sayoko then. I sent a reply by return post, saying we would definitely like her to go ahead. In the meantime, I sent Shino to collect her at Uncle Katsu's on January the tenth, as planned.

Sayoko stayed with us for ten days or so. In the meantime, Shino took her for an interview at the nylon sock factory, and they reached an informal agreement on hiring her.

"That's good news," I said.

"Yes," said Sayoko. "Sorry to have caused you so much worry."

"Do your best until you leave to get married."

"What? I'll never marry!!"

One day, Sayoko moved into the factory dormitory, leaving her vivacious laughter echoing behind her.

On New Year's Day, I had felt the urge to start writing a new story. Our baby was due about six months later. I was unlikely to be of any help to Shino in my present circumstances, so I'd accepted my mother's suggestion that the child be born in my hometown. This new story would then be a good indication of how well I could fend for myself alone, once Shino had left for the country. If I could allow myself just a little optimism, perhaps it might even earn enough money for Shino's journey as well as the hospital costs.

Day and night I sat at my desk immersed in my writing. The narrative progressed in painfully slow stages, but did move steadily on toward its conclusion. At the beginning of February, working long into the night, I forgot to refill the heater with charcoal, and succeeded in catching a cold. Whether that was the cause I don't know, but about four days later, when I thought the cold had subsided, I suddenly developed a fever of 103.

Thinking that my cold had returned, I stayed in bed without working for two days, then a third. But even when the cold symptoms had completely disappeared, the fever remained and showed no sign of abating. Soon, the back of my head started to throb with pain. I normally avoided doctors but felt so wretched this time that I took myself to the local clinic. The doctor's diagnosis on initial examination was a recurrence of my cold, so he gave me an injection and a powdered cold remedy. The powder was soon gone, yet my temperature refused to diminish even slightly. Now the doctor examined me more thoroughly but still could find nothing wrong with me. The only thing for me, he concluded, was to try some medicine capsules called "chloromycetin."

Considering our circumstances, the capsules were very expensive. To make matters worse, I was expected to take one of them every six hours. I had a friend in Mejiro who had bailed me out a number of times in the past. I explained my predicament to him, borrowed the money, and bought the medicine.

My friend in Mejiro came to check on my progress every other day. Other friends from university days, hearing the news from him, came visiting sporadically. They sat at my bedside, offering guesses at the nature of my illness. One said it was tuberculosis, another thought it might be a disease called Izumi fever. One gave me a fright by saying, "It's cholera, isn't it?" Because of the persistent pain at the back of my head, I was tormented by the idea that it might be some kind of disease of the brain. Fevers with no known cause or name are very distressing. I was ready to resign myself to just about any incurable disease if only this uncertainty would disappear; the prospect of brain disease alone was one that I could not face.

The fever started to abate, although very slightly, the day after I started taking the capsules. The pain at the back of my head now also eased with each passing day, and after another ten days I was even able to joke about it. "At last I know what my illness is called," I said to my friends when they came visiting. "The scientific name is Russian for 'poor fever.' They say Dostoevsky had it. From Russia it spread to Europe, where it infected Charles Louis Philippe, among others . . ."

While I was still in the grip of the fever, I would look forward to Sundays most of all. That was when Sayoko came visiting. It was as if my emotions, sodden through with a febrile disease of unknown name, started to warm and dry out again when touched by Sayoko's healthy optimism.

Sayoko would kneel beside my mattress and report on her day-to-day life. For her, even getting up in the morning and brushing her teeth was fun. She would greet her roommates with a hearty "Good morning!" They would raise three fingers at each other and giggle. Just three days to go till Sunday! On Saturday night, she couldn't sleep at all. Watching her roommates eagerly curling their hair as they waited for their sweethearts, she couldn't stop laughing. And on Sunday morning, she was so excited that she'd gone to the toilet three times. She'd fidgeted impatiently on the tram, opened our front door with gusto, and called "Ta-ra!" to her brother-in-law, who had an ice pack on his forehead and was looking drowsy. This recounting of events was shouted rather than spoken by Sayoko. As I listened, in my feverish head I felt a hazy sense of nostalgia for those innocent days when I too could enjoy such a life—a life that I had left behind long ago.

One day, after thus prattling on at random as usual, Sayoko placed a long, thin envelope on the floor inside the doorway as she left. "Here. A get-well letter," she said, before scampering off.

Shino picked up the envelope and looked inside. "Goodness!" she gasped.

It contained a savings passbook and a letter. The balance recorded in the passbook was a truly astonishing amount for an eighteen-year-old to have saved. I read the letter:

Dear Brother,

This is the money I've saved up from brooms, tonkatsu, and nylon socks. I've been saving it because I want to have my own shop selling shiruko sweet bean soup one day. But I'm still only eighteen and I don't need it yet. So I'm giving it to you as a get-well present. Please use it as you like.

—Sayoko

"Well. Isn't she an odd one," I said with deliberate coarseness, thinking inwardly that this was surely the end for me. Here was I, full of high hopes but unable to produce a single thing of worth, yet my own sister-in-law, working at the age of eighteen, had given me her savings passbook. Was my life really worth continuing to the point of using up all her savings as well?

The following Sunday, as always, Sayoko came by with her cheery "Ta-ra!"

"Thank you for your kindness last week," I said. "I appreciate the thought, but I can't possibly accept. You should look after this."

As I went to hand her the passbook, Sayoko rested her forehead against the doorpost and began to cry. Shino and I simply watched in silence. Suddenly, Sayoko turned to face us. "How can you be so heartless?" she said angrily. "That's exactly what's wrong with you! We're supposed to be related, aren't we?! You do nothing but criticize us, but it's *you* who don't treat *us* like family! What a joke!"

Her words hit me hard. Feeling my temper building up inside, I threw the passbook down on the desk.

"All right, I'll keep it. Please don't cry."

I turned over to face the empty bookcase.

At the beginning of March I was finally able to get out of bed. I'd been tormented by fever for a whole month. When I tried to get up, I felt light-headed, and when I tried to walk, my knees seemed about to give. My whole body felt weak and shaky. It was as if the fever had dissolved the very core of my being.

The night sweats continued. Some nights I had to change my bedclothes twice. During prolonged spells of cloudy weather, when no laundry would dry, I would have no clean nightwear left, and would borrow Shino's undergarments to wear in bed. I also suffered from occasional dizziness and palpitations. I made a tremendous effort to sit at my desk, but was simply unable to complete what I'd been writing before my illness. Perhaps the fever had altered the very tissue of my brain cells. Late one night, as I sat there vacantly, the break in my narrative staring me in the face, I heard a clattering sound outside. The local bath attendant was casually hurling water basins across the tiled floor of the bathhouse. Mesmerized by the sound, I flopped down onto my desk and burst into tears.

Now in the latter stages of pregnancy, Shino started complaining of dull pains in her belly. On examining her, the doctor said there was a risk of a premature delivery and gave her an injection of progesterone. The baby could well arrive before the due date in July, he said. His advice was that, if Shino needed to go to the country at all, she should go as soon as possible.

On April the first, I had an announcement for her.

"Look, I think I'll go back with you after all," I said. "You never know what might happen, with me in this condition. We've only been able to put up with all this until now because we've both been healthy. Remember the Kunugi couple? Let's do what they did. Do the wise thing and go back to the country for a while. There's something I want to write, something that's not written for money. I want to take time writing it while gradually getting my health back. Then, when the baby's born, I can make a fresh start. And when I start again, I won't rush anything. I'll try to do better next time."

"Really?" said my wife with a gleam of joy in her eye. "It's not an April Fool's joke?"

We decided to leave on April the tenth.

We borrowed Sayoko's savings to clear our pawned possessions. We scraped our last things together to pay off our back rent. We sold our chests, bookcases and kitchen cupboards, now completely bare, to a secondhand furniture merchant. He even "threw in" my writing desk, although one of its legs was false. All that remained were two small cloth-wrapped bundles, and the broom we'd been given by Kaname. After two years of bitter hardship, we would leave Tokyo with nothing to our name but a wooden broom.

On the morning of our last day, we had a visit from a neighbor, a woman we knew in passing. We had hardly socialized with our neighbors at all, but we always exchanged greetings with this woman when we ran into her on the street. Without any undue embellishment, she held out a flat paper parcel.

"Here are some things for the baby to wear," she said. "I've been working at them for a while, since I wanted to finish them before you left. I'm always dead by nine in the evening, but I managed to finish them last night. Well, they're nothing, really."

"Oh, well, thank you so much, you really shouldn't have . . . and anyway, we don't know if it's a boy or a girl yet," I babbled, staggered at the unexpectedness of it.

"No, they're for any newborn baby, so they'll suit both. Well, take care of yourselves, now," she said as she left.

We opened the paper parcel to find two pure white baby suits inside.

"They'll make a nice keepsake," I said.

"Yes." Shino nodded, her eyes wet with emotion.

A sprinkling of snow had fallen in a tie-dye pattern on the forest beside the railway line. As we passed through a tunnel, the train crossed a junction and started to sway.

"It was snowing the first time we came home, wasn't it?" said Shino.

"So it was. Let's go back to the way we felt then. Let's make a fresh start."

Carrying our little cloth-wrapped bundles and our broom, we stepped out onto the deck of the carriage. Flurries of snow blew at us from the side.

Face of Death

IN THE PAST, whenever I learned of a death in my family, I would find myself gripped by a sense of shame. Death to me was a kind of disgrace. So far, I've lost two sisters to death, and I have two brothers who may or may not still be alive. Their deaths, their misfortunes have all brought shame on our family.

When I was about ten years old, I thought that dying meant committing suicide. Two of my sisters had proved the point. The eldest swallowed poison; the next eldest drowned herself. I was never told the exact details. In my hometown, I was known as the brother of the girl who'd poisoned herself, the boy from the family of the girl who'd drowned herself. It was humiliating. I was scared of other boys my age and always walked along the back streets. But the back-street boys were all the more brash and abusive. So I started making a detour around the town and walking through the fields.

It was while I was walking through the fields on my way to

school one day that I learned of my eldest brother's indiscretion. My brother was a member of the school's Parents' Association, and the school had asked after his whereabouts. Walking through the fields the following morning, I opened and read the reply my father had written. My brother had gone missing, it said. I heard later that he'd gone on a journey with the intention of killing himself, and, on his way, had sent his expensive silk half-coat and stiff obi to his impoverished lover as a keepsake. My head was reeling as I tried to make sense of the letter. There was no one else in the field, and yet I felt so ashamed that I didn't know where to hide. I crumpled up the letter and threw it into a stream, then made myself keep walking as the smoke of a field bonfire filled my throat.

Even then, I was convinced that if I had to die at all, suicide would be the only way, however shameful it might be. I knew no other way. I secretly discovered several methods of committing suicide that no one else knew, but in my excitement I found it hard to choose between them. Then, much to my surprise, we entered a strange era in which suicide was actually glorified.

For me, the war was a perfect opportunity to vindicate the blackened honor of my siblings. I seriously thought my time to die had come. But I was only fifteen and hadn't quite reached the age when I could volunteer for an honorable suicide. I hoped, at the very least, to perish at the hands of the enemy. That summer, the enemy raided our town from the air and came to attack me. If only I'd been doing the usual thing in the usual place, I would have succeeded in dying as I had wished, but a caprice of fate prevented that. Then, one day, the perfect opportunity slipped away altogether.

After the war, I became a young man and began to see that dying did not necessarily mean committing suicide. Even so, I still found it hard to shake off my sense of shame. When I saw people saddened by the death of a relative, I found it odd.

Is it sad when someone dies?

If your father died, would you cry?

I asked myself these kinds of questions and could find no answers. When I met a friend who'd lost a relative, I would bow politely but would not otherwise touch on his misfortune. To me, that seemed the best way to show sympathy.

At the age of eighteen, I went to Tokyo and met my second eldest brother. He took care of me and helped me get into university, but just a year later, he ran off with our family fortune and disappeared. My shame shook me to the very core. It was not only the shame of my family's dishonor, but also that of our folly in trusting him, never once thinking that he might betray us in that way. And it was the shame of my own stupidity, having lived in the same city and seen him often, yet never having had any inkling of his dark ambitions, merely looking up to him as an elder brother and fawning over him. I fled from Tokyo and went roaming around the little hot-spring village where my father had been born, or the fishermen's villages near my hometown, and in this way remained in hiding for three years.

I no longer felt that our misfortunes as siblings were simply the result of circumstance. It was inconceivable that mere circumstance could drive four of us to ruin, one after the other. I wished that one of them, any of them, could have fallen in a normal way. But all of them, without exception, were abnormal.

I thought it must be our blood. I thought that our blood must be the cause of our ruin. If that was so, then the same ruinous blood must also be coursing through my own veins. I would not allow myself to be ruined by my own blood. While feeling ashamed of my blood, I tried to devise ways to live in defiance of it. The simplest way would have been to live in a manner completely opposed to that of my brothers and sisters, and so prevent the fatal lure of my blood in advance. What I eventually did was try to simply accept everything. I even practiced this in minute acts of everyday existence. In everything I did, I tried to think the opposite of what I imagined *they* would think in a given situation, to act altogether differently from how they would act. And when I felt sure that I had mastered this new way of living, I asked my father for some cash and entered university once more.

While I was at university, I met a woman called Shino who worked in a restaurant near my student dormitory, took her back to my hometown and married her there. My brothers and sisters seemed to regard love as something sinful, but I innocently rejoiced in it. Everyone in my family was happy for me. No one put on a false show of airs, and I myself felt ashamed of nothing. It seemed better that way. Our lives may have been poor, but they were normal—my old parents and my sister Kayo in our family home in the country, Shino and I in Tokyo with occasional visits back there. I was now twenty-six.

It was late July. A light drizzle had been falling ever since the morning. Late in the day, a telegram unexpectedly arrived from my northern hometown to say that my father was seriously ill.

At the time, Shino and I were lounging around in our apartment, which faced onto a canal that flowed through the outskirts of Tokyo. We had placed a rose in a glass on top of my empty bookcase and were shooting off its petals one by one with a toy pistol. It was Shino's turn, and as she closed one eye to take aim, she suddenly stopped. "Hey! What's that?" she said. Listening carefully, we could just hear the sound of a motorbike in the distance. We both got up and went over to the window.

A road ran beneath the window. The canal ran along the far side of the road. Beyond that we could see the green motorbike of the telegram deliveryman heading toward us along the foot of a hill. The hill looked like a huge cake, with the white buildings of a housing estate squashed together on top of a slope covered thickly with bamboo grass. Normally, Shino would start to mouth, "This way! This way!" as if she were trying to attract fireflies, and when the motorbike crossed the concrete bridge and turned into the narrow road that ran under our window, she would lean out to receive the telegram through the open window, saying, "It's come, it's come!" I would have to pull one of her arms back inside the room to keep her from falling out. The young deliveryman would give us a dismissive glance as we leaned there at the window. He would continue past us for four or five yards, then deliberately shout "Telegram!" toward the window of another apartment and call my name. That was his way of making us look foolish.

It was a scene that was repeated once or twice a month. We spent our days doing nothing but waiting for telegrams. Although it was already two years since I'd graduated from university, I still had no job, and was scraping a living by writing radio scripts following an introduction by an acquaintance. Once or twice a month I would be called in by a standard telegram bearing the words WORK AVAILABLE. I would collect the work immediately, finish it in a single night and deliver it to the radio station the following day, thereby earning just enough for the two of us to survive for a couple of weeks. If the work had come regularly twice a month, we could have lived more or less like other people, but there were few months that afforded such luxury. If anything, the work had started to slow down since that spring, and in June it petered out altogether. It was worthless work that brought no satisfaction, however often I did it, and I would have liked to be rid of it as soon as possible. But when it stopped coming, we were immediately plunged into hardship. We tried to make ends meet by selling the clothes and furniture Shino had brought with her, as well as every single one of my books, but these soon ran out. I now passed the days immersed in reading a book of *joruri* puppet plays by Chikamatsu, which had only avoided being sold because I'd lent it to a friend.

That day, however, the telegram deliveryman, making what was now a rare appearance, seemed unlike his normal self. He did not glance toward us at the window, but came in through the entrance to the apartments and knocked solemnly on our door.

"Telegram," he called.

When Shino opened the door, he handed her the telegram with a bow, then walked off again, his black vinyl waterproof glistening in the rain. Shino leaned her back against the door and read the telegram, then instantly collapsed in a heap on the tatami mat floor.

In my trepidation, I was unable to pull myself away from the window until the sound of the deliveryman's retreating footsteps could no longer be heard. Then I took the telegram from Shino's lap and read it as I stood.

Father very ill—Come quick

—Kayo

When I first read it through, only the final word made any impression on my mind: Kayo, my one remaining sister. Born with impaired eyesight, she had never set foot in anything like a post office until now. The way she'd written "Come quick" in blunt language instantly conjured up a picture; I imagined her writing those words as she leant on a tilting, rickety ink-stained desk in the gloomy earth-floored room of a country post office, earning curious looks from the post office staff, not knowing that the normal wording was "Urgent" or "Return at once." Spurred by a sense of alarm, I read the telegram again from the beginning, but still my eyes merely glossed over those key three words at the beginning, and I was unable to feel the reality of it.

My father was close to death. I understood that much. And

even I didn't think it was suicide this time. He was already seventy, and had suffered a mild stroke five years earlier. Although he'd made a gradual recovery since then, he could have suffered a relapse at any time. "I won't be around much longer," he would often laugh, only half kidding. "Give me one last push, and I'll drop down dead." Now it seemed that his "last push" had finally arrived.

But there again, what does it mean when we say that someone is "close to death"? Death, surely, comes unexpectedly and disappears again in the same instant, leaving only the body behind. In the past, deaths in my family had been accompanied by the bodies of the deceased. That's how it was with my two sisters. It was also like that for the people who were attacked from the air during the war. By the time we realized that death had come for them, they were already dead bodies. We only knew of a person's death when we saw the body; there was no gap between death and the body. Death came swiftly, and retreated swiftly too. All that was left was for those who remained to hold a somber ceremony in which they gathered around the body and wept.

I found it hard to believe that my father was dying. And so I felt no surprise, no sorrow.

"This is a wretched turn of events," I said toward the gathering gloom of twilight outside the window as I folded the telegram. Shino rose hesitantly to her feet.

"What should we do?"

"What *can* we do? We'll have to go."

It was simple enough to say, but my hometown was near the northern end of Honshu, and we obviously had no savings to pay for our fare up there. And we couldn't just go this time with the clothes on our backs, either. If my father were to die, I would be the chief mourner. Shino would also have to comport herself in front of people in the proper way. But we didn't have a single item of formal clothing on hand. It was still being held by the pawnbroker, and we would need a huge sum of money to get it all back.

I spent an unduly long time gathering everything together. By the time I'd been to three of my friends' houses to borrow the money and had returned with the fare and the clothes, it was already close to midnight. We'd decided to take the northbound express the following morning, and had resigned ourselves to staying up all night when another telegram arrived.

Father worse—Hurry

—Kayo

I stood by the window, the smell of the canal wafting over toward me. I thought I would surely never see my father alive again, and assumed that it was our destiny, as people who shared the same blood, that neither of us could witness the other's death.

In the drizzle, the lamps strung up along the canal appeared as a reddish blur. They looked exactly like the paper lanterns at cherry blossom–viewing time in the country.

It was raining when we reached my hometown late the follow-ing evening. As we walked along the cavernous underpass that led from the platform beneath the tracks and toward the station building, the chilly night air typical of the north country passed over the nape of my neck, even though it was the height of sum-mer. I instinctively braced myself in both body and mind.

Under the dim electric light at the ticket gate, my Christian uncle, who lived in another town, was standing with his umbrella, appearing to hug it in the chest of his black suit. As soon as I saw him standing there, I assumed that my father had died, without knowing why. When my uncle saw us, he came running toward us, his tall rubber boots making squelching noises as he did.

"Sorry to be so late," I said.

"No, you've come so far, it can't be helped," my uncle replied. He said there was some business he had to see to at home that night, and that he was about to leave on the same steam train on which we had arrived. To me, it sounded like an excuse not to attend the wake. "That's all right," I said. "We'll take care of things from here."

At that, he suddenly blinked. "Don't feel bitter, just do what you can," he said. "We all have to go sometime. Everything's in God's hands." The train blew its whistle. "Well, goodbye, then," he said, and then, holding the handle of his umbrella aloft, raced down to the underpass in feverish haste.

The station was deserted at that hour, and only a bewilder-ing number of small insects swirled silently around the electric lamps. No one else was there to meet us. We'd sent a telegram from inside the train, so there could have been no mistaking our time of arrival. I thought perhaps they might all be angry that we'd dallied so long as to miss my father's final moments. The two of us could have made our way home together, but there was a sea of mud outside the station building. I only had ordinary shoes on my feet, while my wife wore a kimono with *zori* sandals. As I vacillated at the station entrance not knowing what to do, a human figure came into view. The figure ran unsteadily toward us along the muddy road, whose deep ruts glistened like railway tracks in the dim light of the street lamps. I thought it might be old Grandma Kaji. We waited for the figure to approach.

Yes, it was Kaji. She was a kind-hearted farmer's widow who lived opposite our house.

"So sorry! So sorry!" she said. "The taxi driver's gone off drinking someplace. He's been ferrying your guests to and fro all day, and he must have made more money than he has in a while. I bet he's gone off to that little restaurant in the next town."

Actually, the old woman's breath also smelt of alcohol. I wondered if perhaps the wake drinking had started already, as I changed into some rubber boots that I'd taken from a cloth bundle hanging at Kaji's back. Shino hiked up her kimono and put on another pair, completely exposing her knees and shins.

"Don't I look a sight?" she said.

"No, you look nice and cool," said Kaji.

We waded through the mud along the main road, which was lined with houses that were already shut up for the night. I wanted to know how and when my father had died, but I couldn't bring myself to ask. It wasn't because we were with Grandma Kaji. I probably couldn't have asked my uncle either. I had a terrible feeling of dread at the thought of hearing, from the mouth of another, the cause of my father's death and the way in which he'd died. It was not a dread of hearing the truth, but a dread of feeling shame.

When I was a child, two of my sisters had died in quick succession, but for some years afterward I remained quite unaware that the first had drowned herself. One day, a blacksmith's son who'd lost an argument with me revealed the truth in front of everyone. "Your sister was eaten by a dolphin off Tsugaru!" he declared.

Suicide was shameful enough, but I felt a different type of shame in being the only person not to know about it when everyone else did. When my second sister died and our house was swept up in confusion, I had no hesitation in asking my mother: "Did she kill herself?"

At that, my mother swiftly took hold of my head and buried it in her chest, weeping pitifully. I grew up too cowardly to hear about death from others, or to ask them about it myself.

Shino said not a word about my father, as if she had also given up hope. We walked past an orchard by the roadside, and she gasped when she saw the wet apples in the orchard shining brightly each time our flashlight passed over them. Beyond the orchard, the sound of the river's flow suddenly grew louder as we reached the bridge.

"Your father used to like fishing, didn't he?" said Grandma Kaji. "He can't fish any more now, of course. But right up until a few days ago, he used to stand on this bridge all the time and watch people fishing. I suppose he won't be doing that so much now."

Feeling a certain warmth in her words, I smiled.

"Well, there must be rivers on the other side, too," I said, intending it as a joke.

"How do you mean?" the old woman asked back sharply.

"I mean, I'll put a fishing rod in my father's coffin."

"What!" she cried, and stopped still. "How could you say something so unlucky? Whoever said your father was dead?"

I was stunned.

"No, no, not yet," she swaggered in a shrill voice. "He's waiting for you to get back first! Come up here expecting to find him dead, what kind of a son are you?"

"Thank goodness!" Shino cried out, then hit me several times in the back with her fist by way of punishment. "Thank goodness! Thank goodness!" she repeated over and over.

My parents' home was brightly lit, both upstairs and down, and the light spilling out of the windows captured the falling spray of summer rain like a searchlight. For a moment, I stopped in my tracks, entranced by this illuminated night view of my home. I could never remember seeing our house look so bright.

My sister Kayo came running to the front door when she heard Grandma Kaji calling loudly, and immediately flung herself around my shoulders. "Were you surprised?" she asked quietly, though her face was smiling.

"Yes," I answered with a smile of my own, still overwhelmed by the brilliance of the house.

Kayo turned to Shino. "You must be tired," she said.

"No, I'm just sorry we're so late," Shino replied.

"It's all right, really it is," said my sister, nodding as she nudged me from behind, pushing me toward the back room.

My father was stretched out under a blanket near the dresser in the twelve-mat room. My mother sat huddled on the floor between the dresser and my father's futon, gripping his right hand with one of her hands and waving a fan with the other. By his pillow sat my aunt, my mother's younger sister, who had married a liquor store owner in the neighboring prefecture.

"We're here," I said as I knelt in the doorway.

"You're here?" asked my mother, wrinkling up her face in joy.

My aunt brought her face down close to my father's. "Look," she said. "He's arrived!"

My father, his face still turned toward my mother, mumbled something inaudible. "What's that?" asked my mother, bringing her ear close to his lips. Then she turned to me. "'Thank you for coming,' he says."

My aunt laughed. "Your mother must be an interpreter—she's the only one who understands a word he says! That's married life for you!"

"He can't turn that way, son, why don't you come over here?" said my mother, beckoning me over with her fan. Still on my knees, I edged forward and peered into his face.

He was a little thinner than when I'd last seen him in the spring, though his face hadn't changed unduly. His eyes and cheeks appeared slightly withdrawn toward the back of his head, but perhaps I was just imagining that. His nose and mouth seemed to be bent toward the cheek that was half pressed down on his pillow. I didn't know if this was due to his illness. Then again, I wouldn't normally look so closely at his face. His complexion didn't seem too bad. His whole face was flushed pink, as if with over-excitement, and moist with perspiration. Part of his forehead was particularly red, as though daubed with crimson ink, a sure sign that he was feeling quite agitated. Ever since he'd collapsed the first time, a welt-like redness would automatically appear on his forehead whenever he felt worked up. His breathing was certainly heavy; his mouth was open and he was gasping. On the whole, nonetheless, it was difficult to imagine that this was a person who was suffering from a serious illness and was on the verge of death.

Even so, it seemed to require considerable effort for him just to alter his line of vision. He slowly turned his eyeballs downward and barely managed to glance at my face. "Father," I called instinctively as our eyes met. To be sure, my tone sounded unnatural, like a child reading from a schoolbook. But now a bashful expression spread around my father's eyes. He stiffened his chin as if he was straining, and gasped fitfully, feverishly with his flattened mouth. That was his way of laughing.

"Well, well, well, look how strong you are now!" my mother said as she shook my father's right hand, which she held in both of her hands above her knee. Looking closely, I noticed that both their arms were shaking violently, as if they were arm wrestling, and I realized for the first time that my mother was not just gripping my father's hand for show. I'd heard that if left to its own devices, his right hand would start making wayward movements of its own accord. Occasionally, a tremendous spasm of strength would pass through it. My mother was obviously struggling to keep the arm pressed down toward her knee.

"It might be best not to excite him too much," my aunt said, then turned to my father. "That's enough now, isn't it? You feel better now, don't you? Why don't you have a nice rest," she said, as if pacifying a simple-minded child.

A deep growl that sounded like a tomcat's purr emanated from my father's throat. My mother put her ear to his mouth and nodded. "He says you're not to worry," she explained, turning to us. "He says you should have a rest now, too."

We withdrew to the living room, where we sat beside the open fire and drank some green tea my sister had made.

"What do you think about Father?" she asked me.

"Actually, it feels odd. He doesn't look that bad after all," I replied.

"Well, you're wrong there—he's not doing well at all. He's finally quieted down now, but we can't become complacent."

Two evenings earlier, a *shakuhachi* teacher called Oda had come over, and was accompanying Kayo as she played her koto upstairs. It would normally have been time for my father to go to bed, but that evening he sat by the fireplace in the living room as he listened to their music-making upstairs.

"What tune is that?" he asked after they'd played a few pieces.

"*Kajimakura*, I think," answered my mother.

"It's a bit long," my father said, then got up and went to the privy. It was his habit to relieve himself before settling down for the night. His chronic constipation had only gotten worse with his illness, and he tended to spend a long time in there.

That evening, he still hadn't come back out even after "Kajimakura" had ended. When my mother noticed and looked at the clock, twenty minutes had already passed. In her concern, she opened the door at the entrance to the privy. "Dad!" she called. "You've been in there for twenty minutes, you know!"

"I know, I know. I'm just coming out now," Father said from inside the privy, as if nothing was wrong. My mother returned to the living room, but five minutes later he still hadn't reappeared. Suddenly struck by a sense of foreboding, she hurried back to the privy. She opened the entrance door and noticed that the inner door was also open. My father was still squatting there, but his body was leaning heavily to the left.

"Dad!" my mother called, almost shouting.

"Don't worry. What's up? What's up?" my father mumbled inarticulately and laughed. But his body remained leaning there and would not budge. Startled, my mother called Mr. Oda from upstairs, and he and my sister helped to carry Father to his bed. His body was as heavy as a thick log of wood soaked in water.

My sister appeared to have related this story to my father's visitors many times over, and seemed quite accustomed to telling it, for she did so without once faltering. She also used the correct term for his illness—encephalomalacia, softening of the brain. Suddenly, she lowered her voice.

"My telegram was funny, wasn't it?"

"No," I replied, "not particularly."

"I don't know how to write them, you see. It was the first time I'd ever sent one. When I told Mr. Oda that, he just laughed at me."

Kayo, thirty-six years old and still unmarried, blushed and giggled like a little girl. It seemed there was nothing she wouldn't tell Mr. Oda.

My aunt entered the living room. She told Kayo that Mother was calling her, and then, when my sister had left the room, sat down in the spot she had just vacated.

"You must be really tired," my aunt said to Shino, as if to console her. Then she turned to me. "This may be the end for your father," she said with an air of nonchalance.

"Yes," I agreed.

"If only your brothers were here . . ."

I said nothing.

"He must want to see them, too, after all. If not Bunzo, Takuji could make the effort, surely," my aunt said ruefully.

In truth, I'd already given up on my brothers. It was twenty years since my eldest brother Bunzo had set out on his "journey of death," and seven since my second brother Takuji had departed on his voyage of betrayal. In the meantime, there'd been no word from either of them, and we didn't even know if they were dead or alive. But even if they were alive and knew that our father was close to death, there was surely no chance, judging from their natures, that they would meekly rush home now. They were the ones who had discarded us. We'd lived our lives thinking that there was a special way of living for people who had been discarded. There was no longer any room in our lives for them to return.

"Forget about my brothers. I'm sure Father wouldn't want to see them. Even my mother—" I started to say, but then suddenly felt a presence behind me. When I turned to look, my mother was standing quietly in the doorway, unnoticed by everyone.

From that night on, we divided ourselves into two groups—me with my mother, Shino with my sister—and took turns watching over my father for two-hour shifts through the night. One of us sat between his futon and the dresser, holding his right hand, while the other fanned the air over him.

When I took hold of my father's hand, I realized that the rest of his body was already beyond his control. His left arm and lower body were not moving at all, as if they were already dead. There was hardly any movement in his lips or eyelids either. He was able to communicate his wishes, faintly, by using his lower right arm from the elbow down, although that too moved randomly of its own accord. When I gripped his fingers, he gripped back with an uncanny strength. If we lightly held his arm down and let him control the hand, he would desperately grope with his fingers at the chest of the person helping him. At other times he would make vigorous attempts to pinch his chin with the sides of his thumb and index finger.

At first I assumed that this behavior of my father's hand was entirely the result of nervous spasms caused by his illness; but once, when his hand had finished undoing all the buttons on my shirt from the top down after a tremendous effort, I realized that this was my father's last remaining resistance against his illness, his own desperate prayer for recovery. From that time on,

I deliberately let his hand do what he wanted it to. If he tried to grab my Adam's apple, I would let him do it and forego swallowing. If he tried to grab my nose, I would simply hold my breath and wait.

In the middle of the night, as I dozed next to my father, I was awoken by Shino calling his name. I looked up to see his hand touching her nipple through her dress as if poking it, stroking it as if brushing it, and in the end pinching it between his two fingers. Even then, Shino didn't move away, but chided him quietly and smiled in embarrassment. To me, that was the most affectionate scene my father had ever performed with his children until now. With that thought, I then fell back to sleep. There were several nights like that.

In the afternoon of the day after our arrival, a doctor from the prefectural hospital came by on a house call. He asked me if we could have an informal chat, which we did in the next room. The doctor said that this week would be decisive, but that with my father's disease, the blood vessels in the brain are ruptured one after the other—a process invisible to the naked eye—and that we should therefore be prepared for the worst to happen at any moment. It sounded like a death sentence. Again, my father's nephew, a man who was a parish councilor or something, came visiting. "Well, if you ask me, Uncle won't last until the Bon festival," he said complacently. I wouldn't know for sure that my father was dead unless I could see it with my own eyes. Predictions of death were meaningless to me. I was angered, nonetheless, by people's blithe lack of concern. It's easy for a doctor to high-handedly threaten doom in a loud, booming voice that can easily be heard by the patient. And a villager from a wealthy family may well fear lung disease as if it were cholera, but when it comes to encephalomalacia, chat idly and say, "He's got it!" Both of them treated my father as if he was already dead; in other words, they treated him with equal contempt. I got up and left them without a word.

In the early evening my aunt had to go home. When she took her leave of my father, he mistook it as meaning that we would also be returning to Tokyo, and grew distraught. My mother managed to persuade him that we weren't leaving, but he remained agitated. After that, he started to call my mother and ask my whereabouts whenever he could not actually see me. I had to remain within his tiny field of vision all day, and especially at night. For my father was as scared of the night as a small child would be.

Late one night, while I was holding my father's hand, he made a sign that he wanted me to bend my ear to him. He then proceeded to speak to me, carefully shaping his lips to pronounce each word. His speech, interspersed with a sound like a poorly blown whistle, reached my ear punctuated with frequent pauses.

"When . . . are you . . . going . . . home?" he asked first.

I replied that I was not.

"What . . . about . . . your work?" he asked.

My father was the only one who believed steadfastly in the work that I'd continued since my student days, work that hadn't the remotest prospect of finding reward. If I were to self-deprecatingly make light of that work, my father would arch his eyebrows, rebuke me for my indolence, and slump his shoulders disconsolately. And yet even that work, however insignificant, would soon be buried in the abyss of our impoverished lives. If my father had known that the only thing left in my suitcase was a book of *joruri* puppet plays by Chikamatsu, he would have been so disappointed that he might well have dropped dead on the spot. Though I felt pain in my heart, I replied that it was all right, I'd brought a lot of work home with me.

"I'll be around . . . for a while . . . you know," my father said.

Up until that point, I'm sure he'd intended to live a long time. When I told him that that was fine with me, he stared languidly at my face, his eyes filled with light from the electric lamp.

"Really?" he asked at length, as if to make sure.

For a short while, I was unable to move my ear from his lips, and in that pose I watched as my father's bony chest heaved violently. The depth of my father's mistrust was truly pitiful. Pitiful was the heart of a man who had fathered six children, four of whom had betrayed him in turn while they were still young, a father who even now couldn't bring himself to trust me, his only remaining son. Feeling an unbearable sadness, I said nothing but shook his hand firmly. With that, calm spread over his features.

"All right . . . All right."

I'm sure that's what he said. Then he half-closed his eyes and fell asleep immediately, snoring with astonishing intensity.

Naturally my father's condition worsened by the day. The strength of his grip gradually weakened, and he soon lost the energy to grope at our chests. His tongue grew increasingly stiff, and he could no longer even drink the small quantities of liquid food that he'd managed until then. The only thing he could do was to sip cold *hojicha* tea, but he choked even on that and brought it up again most of the time. The occasional word that would slip from his lips could no longer be heard easily, even by my mother.

On the fourth day, all expression vanished from his face. Only when we were cleaning up after a call of nature would he knit his brows in evident discomfort. Whenever we changed his underclothes, it was my job to straddle his belly, my back to him, and lift both his knees. His body no longer bore the slightest resemblance to the man he had once been—a man who, at five foot ten and 150 pounds, was the sturdily built son of a rich farmer, had learned judo at secondary school and then, by the age of twenty, had married into the family of my mother, the eldest daughter of a well-established kimono merchant. He had never been especially quick, but he was so rapidly and often shuttled between various shop clerks in his apprenticeships that he soon developed an aversion to local commerce. Then one day out of the blue he declared, "I'm going to Tokyo to become a sumo wrestler," which made my mother cry. When I went to hold this man's legs, his blackened skin floated over the top of his bones, and when I lifted those legs, they rose straight up into the air with but the slightest effort.

On the fifth day, his throat began to growl constantly. It was phlegm. Phlegm had gradually started to appear some time earlier, but on the fifth day it suddenly increased. My father no longer had the strength to cough it up. Peering into his mouth, I could see his tongue bulged into a cylindrical shape that was purple in color and stuck to his lower gums. Meanwhile, a clump of advancing phlegm was lodged at the back of his throat, forming a milky white film that threatened to block his windpipe. Each time he breathed, his throat would make a gravelly, rasping sound.

With encephalomalacia, they say the end is near when phlegm appears. The visiting doctor took one glance inside my father's mouth, frowned, and folded his arms as if giving up, then looked back over his shoulder at the childlike nurse who had accompanied him. "Give them instructions on how to remove the phlegm," he said. The nurse asked for a pair of chopsticks and held one of them up. "Er, this is to make sure he doesn't bite his tongue," she explained, placing it sideways inside my father's mouth. Then she wrapped cotton wool around the end of the other chopstick. "And, er, with this one you swab the phlegm and take it out," she continued. She placed the second chopstick inside my father's mouth and twirled it around, then took it out again and shrieked. The cotton wool she'd placed at the end of the chopstick was no longer there. "Idiot!" the doctor scolded her. He twirled the chopstick into the throat himself and finally retrieved the cotton wool. He said something like, "Anyway, make sure you do it correctly," gave my father an injection of heart stimulant to maintain appearances, and left.

When we actually tried to do as the nurse had explained, however, we realized that we were in no position to fault her for her failed attempt. A thick, viscous film of phlegm stuck fast to the folds in my father's throat like a living thing with tentacles. It rattled and moved every time he breathed, making it very difficult to scoop it onto the cotton wool from a distance and remove it. I felt sure that my father's throat would immediately become blocked by a heavy mass of phlegm if we didn't continue to clear it for him frequently. Since my mother and sister both had impaired vision, Shino and I had to take care of this task. We pulled up several threads of phlegm each about a foot long and linked together like strings of beads, but still more and more phlegm kept rising up endlessly. Because his mouth was continuously kept open for long periods, my father's eyes soon filled with tears.

"Don't give up, Dad. I'll pull out as much as I can," Shino said to encourage him, as she adroitly removed another two strings of phlegm. "Look Dad, look how much I've got out," she said, showing them to him.

"Thank you, Shino. Thank you," he said loudly and incredibly clearly, as if he'd been saving the words just for that moment.

And the tears flowed out of his eyes, down toward his ears.

For a moment, I wondered if I'd misheard him, but Shino stared in surprise. Then she got up quickly, as if she'd been struck, covered her face with her hands, and ran from the room crying.

Those final two strings of phlegm were the last we could manage for my father. He could no longer either close his mouth or swallow, and because he was breathing so heavily, the inside of his mouth dried quickly and the phlegm merely increased in viscosity. The surface of his tongue was now completely parched and starting to crack. The cracks would start to bleed with even the slightest impact, causing my father such pain that he would wave his hand to indicate "Enough." The back of his throat was like the inside of a limestone cave. Though occasionally taken by the urge to relieve the back of his throat with our fingers, we had to continually moisten his tongue, which was cracked like a rice field in drought, by putting water on the end of the chopstick that was supposed to be used for removing phlegm.

My father weakened visibly. It was as if he could clearly feel his end approaching, for a kind of energy that resembled now impatience, now anguish—distressing for everyone watching—could be felt coming from his motionless body. He started to complain of headaches and to say things like "fireworks" in apparent delirium. I wondered if perhaps he could see images of the capillary vessels in his brain bursting like sparklers, projected onto his dark retinas.

The doctor came that evening. "There's nothing more I can do," he said bluntly. He gave him an injection of camphor, and had some oxygen breathing apparatus brought over, but this was just a last hopeless throw of the dice. My father did make a final show of resistance when the black rubber tube was inserted into his nostrils, but the nurse easily controlled him with her hand and stuck the rubber tube to his forehead and the bridge of his nose with something that looked like cellophane tape.

That night, we all sat around his sickbed and continued to watch over Father. A wind started to blow, making the chimes on the eaves of the roof ring through the night.

It was the next morning, the morning of August the fourth.

My father's breathing had slowed considerably. His chest heaved and wheezed, but his breathing was so weak as to be almost nonexistent. His eyes were fixed in one direction and would not move, while his hands and feet were now cold.

My mother called him loudly two or three times, but he showed no reaction at all.

"Dad's leaving us," she said. "Everyone call him, will you? Please call him."

"Dad! Dad!" Kayo and Shino called as they clung to my father's body.

My mother quietly patted his heaving chest with the palm of her hand and spoke as if reasoning with him. "Dad, you can leave us in peace now. We'll look after ourselves all right. You can leave this life in peace." A flood of tears fell onto the palms of her hands. This struck me as strange—she was telling him to depart this life even while he was still breathing. For his sake, I was ashamed of my mother's apparent haste.

"Mother, please don't say that," I said. "He's still . . ."

"But, son . . ." she started to say, as tears dripped from the end of her nose. She stopped herself and withdrew her hand from his chest.

In that instant, my father had died.

The women threw themselves upon his body and wept. I leaned back against the dresser, fixed my stare on the space above my father, and listened hard. I was poised, ready to capture with my various senses any event, however small, that might occur above his body in the next few moments. But there was nothing. All that happened was that some brightly shining substance came welling up from inside his mouth. It was phlegm. That mass of accumulated phlegm that had so stubbornly refused to move and had caused my father such suffering was now nothing more than a floppy liquid that sparkled in the light of morning as it attempted to leave his body. It exactly resembled the retreat of the devil's agent who, now relieved of his sole duty, tries to return to base.

So that's what death is, I thought, as I sat entranced by the sparkle of the phlegm, which now flowed over the stubble that seemed suddenly to have grown on my father's chin. He had become the first of my kin to die a normal death. Whether we seek death or it seeks us, and whenever, wherever, for whatever reason we may die, it seemed to me that death, which arrives and leaves in a fraction of a second, is exactly the same for everyone. No death can ever be beautiful or ugly. One day, death comes and departs again instantly, leaving only a dead body behind. It is so astonishingly cold, so awfully austere. It offers no room at all for any emotion to slip through. It doesn't even want to accept sadness immediately. That made me wonder about the shame I'd felt each time someone had died until now. I concluded that my shame was merely the result of an illusion arising from my sense of inferiority about my blood. In the face of death, all illusions disintegrate. In fact, my usual sense of shame simply failed to appear.

It was strange nonetheless that a vibrant expression returned to my father's face, conversely, once he had died. Every now and then I went back to see his body, which lay with his head pointing northward in the customary manner. I was captivated when I lifted the white cloth that covered his face. With each passing moment, a miraculous transformation was occurring there. First, his facial expression, distorted with the suffering of his struggle against disease, gradually relaxed. The face then became white and finally started to take on color.

It was a trick played by death. A strange expression of tranquility that I'd never seen before came over his features. His face showed no trace of the various emotions that had tormented him over his seventy years—shame, sorrow, regret, self-reproach, prayer, resignation, and others that were surely strangers to comfort. Even knowing that this was a trick, I couldn't help feeling a flood of emotions, particularly remorse. As I gazed at my father's dead face, now transformed into the exact likeness of an old man's Noh mask, it struck me that if that face had ever held such rich expression while my father was still alive, then the sins of his first four children had painted over it with dishonor. The shame of knowing that my father had had to live his entire life with that dishonor was mine. Death had relieved him of any dishonor, but my shame would remain.

I realized at last that my father really had fallen into the hands of death. I was struck by an inexpressible sadness, and only then did my tears begin to fall.

Magic Lantern Show

EIGHT-YEAR-OLD ORIN tightened her cheeks to form dimples, made a sucking sound and announced, "I've got syphilis."

"Oh. Does it feel good?" I asked, squatting close to her face. I was six.

"How could it feel good? It's a poison. A horrible poison. It lives inside my body."

Orin opened her eyes wide but didn't seem even a little bit sad. I was not satisfied with that, so I gave her white thighs a pinch.

"Ow!"

"You say a horrible poison's living inside you, but you don't look the tiniest bit sad!"

"I am. I'm sad," she said, suddenly frowning.

"If you're sad, how come you're not crying?"

"All right, I will cry! Just stop pinching me!"

Orin thrust out her lower lip and started to sob. When I saw her mouth fill with saliva that began to ooze out in a long thread from a gap between her decayed baby teeth, I was satisfied.

"You can stop crying now."

Orin instantly stopped crying and wiped her mouth with the hem of her short kimono. As she did, I caught sight of her unnaturally swollen abdomen sticking out above her skinny thighs. It reflected the color of the moss on the ground and looked like a frog's belly.

"If that poison is living inside your fat tummy, how did it get in there?" I asked more sympathetically.

"It didn't get in there, I was born with it. Here, look at my fingernails. They're all cracked lengthwise, see? They say that's a sign of syphilis. And when people with syphilis grow up, their noses fall off."

Orin opened her eyes wide again, and actually seemed to be speaking with pride. I stared at Orin's primly upturned nose. Why would it fall off?

"Liar! Who says so?"

"My mom says so. She says my first mom was no good."

"You got two moms?"

"Yeah. But my first mom went over the Mabechi River and over the mountains, far far away, and left me. So now I only got one."

That was her stepmother, a woman with dark-edged eyes who spoke in a rasping voice.

"Will you still marry me anyway?" Orin asked.

"Yes."

I'd said it many times before.

"Even if my nose falls off?"

"Yes. Even if your nose falls off."

"What will you give me when we're married?"

"A neckpiece for a kimono."

"What color?"

"Peach."

Orin stood up briskly. Having confirmed that the color of the neckpiece I would give her was peach, she would always stand up briskly. Then she would hurry off home without even saying goodbye, as if to pursue the phantom of that neckpiece.

My family ran a kimono shop, the second building from the corner of the main street. I was the third son, the last of six children. My brothers and sisters were all much older than me; even my closest sister was ten years my senior. The first five children in my family were all born about a year apart, but I arrived much later, like a careless afterthought.

None of my brothers or sisters lived at home. The only people who lived in our house were my parents and me, a maid and two apprentices.

Orin was my only playmate. Her father ran a bean-jam cake stall beside the service entrance to a concrete-walled bank next to our house. One day as I was standing by our shop window, Orin came sidling up and pressed her face against the glass.

"What's that?" she asked.

"A neckpiece for a kimono," I replied.

After that, Orin came to see the neckpiece every day. In the process, she would tell me about her syphilis, make me promise to marry her, then return home. It was a daily routine that was set in stone. When Orin went home, I felt as if the day had ended. And in this way, when I was six, I lived a life of tranquil contentment with my family.

In the spring when I was seven, on a morning when a March wind blew, I was watching one of the apprentices, Goro, enjoying a puff on my father's cigarette butt in the shop, when a policeman suddenly stepped in. Goro hurriedly hid the cigarette in the ashes of the brazier and stood up.

"Is this where Mina lives?" asked the policeman, glancing at his notebook. Goro said nothing, but merely ducked his head obsequiously and went out to the back as if intending to escape. When my mother came out from the back room, the policeman bowed to her and repeated the same question.

"Yes," my mother replied, "Mina is my second daughter."

The policeman blinked nervously. "Actually . . ." he said, then suddenly glared at me and closed his mouth. I shuddered in fright and ran to the back of the shop. As I turned to steal a furtive look through a gap in the wooden lattice surrounding the cash desk, I saw my mother crumple into a heap in front of the policeman.

I stopped instinctively. The policeman, catching sight of me, beckoned wildly. "You there! Call your father, quick!" he yelled. I was about to go into the back room when my mother, who'd been slumped on the floor, stood upright again as if nothing had happened.

"Thank you for letting us know," she said to the policeman, but once he'd left, she slumped back down onto the floor with her arms around her knees.

After that, a whirlwind visited our house.

Each time the wind blew down our street, whipping up clouds of dust as it went, the special black and white curtains that had been hung all over the shop front would flap and flutter, or cling fast to the glass door. People I'd never seen before would enter with downcast faces through the part where the curtains were gathered up. Some of them I recognized, but they paid me even less attention than usual.

"What's happening?" I would ask.

"Nothing. Nothing. Later," they would all reply before entering the Buddhist altar room.

In the altar room, incense was burning. A priest came and chanted sutras.

The nanny told me that someone had died.

Two days later, a funeral procession set out from my house in the afternoon. The nanny took my hand and we followed the procession to a temple.

Inside the temple, a world of mystery presented itself. As I listened to the strange music and the monks' voices droning on under the dazzling reflections of light, I began to feel as if I was dreaming. I went to stand before the altar with my mother, cast some brown powder into a fire, and put my hands together in prayer.

Above the altar hung a large framed photograph. When I saw it, I instinctively smiled at the person in the photograph. It was my middle sister Mina. Her hair was plaited and hung down on either side of her neck. She always wore purple *hakama* culottes. My mother pulled my sleeve and we returned to our places.

"Don't smile!" chided my second brother, who had come back from Tokyo.

When the ceremony seemed all but over, an old man in a formal kimono stepped forward and spoke to my father in whispers. Then he bowed to us politely and went to stand in front of the altar.

"Mina. Why did you die?" he cried suddenly, as if rebuking her. The old man's body seemed to make great swaying movements to and fro.

"Mina. Why did you say nothing to me?" he said with chin wobbling. "Were you and I not companions in poetry?" he added, his voice suddenly reduced to a murmur. He stood there for a moment with his head hung low. People all around us began to cry.

A stiff wind was blowing when we reached the cemetery. The wooden grave markers all quivered under its force. Our procession, led by a boy priest carrying a bell, continued along a narrow, winding stone path that led to the new grave. Each time the huge paulownia branches groaned in the wind, the sound of the bell would break off abruptly and the boy would strike the bell in silence. I remember seeing, high above the tops of the trees, a solitary red kite hanging motionless in the sky, as if the sky held it fast.

I sensed that my family was afraid to tell me of Mina's death. Overpowered by the curiously secretive silence that reigned over our house, I felt little inclination to ask about it either.

My father would silently work his abacus behind the wooden

lattice grille around the cash desk. Occasionally, he would clear his throat gruffly and cough up phlegm. Sometimes he would lift me up, but would then merely place his nose against my cheek, say "You smell of milk," and put me down again immediately.

My mother, her eyes reddened, seemed distracted most of the time, but then would scold me hysterically without warning.

In a district not far from our house was a department store that my uncle owned. At sunset, the glass windows of the observatory on its roof, visible from the courtyard of our house, seemed to burn brilliantly as if on fire. Right behind the department store stood my uncle's house, which we called "the big house." It was my mother's family home. My uncle was her younger brother.

My eldest brother Fumiya not only worked as my uncle's assistant but also lived in the big house, so that he could learn all about running a business.

He was as thin as a rake, tall with an unnaturally small face. He used to wear a black kimono fastened with a stiff obi waist sash. Every now and then, he would suffer long fits of weak coughing. And that was all I knew about him.

At first, I didn't even know who he was or how he was related to me. So I furtively asked the old clerk at the big house, much to his amusement. He told me that Fumiya was my eldest brother. "Oh," I thought. Not only were we so distant in age as to be father and son, but I had no memory of living in the same house as him, and certainly had never entertained the notion that we were of the same blood.

Once, in the drawing room of my uncle's house, the two of us ate dinner together.

We were eating deep-fried shrimp. I picked one up with my chopsticks and bit into it with gusto.

"Could you eat a little more slowly?" my brother asked irritably. I nodded and bit my shrimp more gently, then put the remainder back onto the same dish. "Don't put food back once you've started eating it!" he said, more angrily this time, his eyes flashing behind his long lashes. I nodded again, but old habits don't change so quickly. No sooner had he spoken than I did the same thing again. When I realized and looked up at his face, I met his withering look and couldn't help giggling nervously at my own stupidity.

Blue veins stood out conspicuously on his receding white forehead. He gripped his red lacquered chopstick case with a shaking hand and struck me hard on the head without a word.

Apart from that incident, his image has entirely vanished from my memory. I remembered his appearance each time I saw a heron in a picture book, but I still couldn't even remember his name.

My second brother Takuji lived in Tokyo, and would come home at the end of each year. He'd studied applied chemistry at technical college and now worked as an engineer in a research institute.

One morning, when my second brother was due to come home, the nanny took me to meet him at the station. My second brother was scarcely better known to me than the eldest, but I still vaguely remembered his face.

When the train pulled in, I had no trouble finding someone who looked like my second brother among the passengers who stepped out onto the platform. Chin buried deep in the collar of his overcoat, he came through the ticket gate blowing clouds of chilly white breath. As he approached us, I suddenly felt overcome by an odd emotion that I didn't fully understand, and simply turned my back on him. While he was still among a group of people, I recognized him without hesitation as my own kin, but when I saw him close-up as we waited there, I was struck with the sensation that he was a complete and utter stranger to me.

My brother could never remember me well, as I was changing so much each year, while my nanny had never met him and was entirely dependent on my hazy memory.

"He didn't come," I muttered morosely, and felt truly disillusioned as I followed my brother, who had walked on ahead with eyes cast down, his body leaning slightly toward his brown trunk.

On our arrival, my mother sat me on my brother's knee. "Didn't you recognize him?" she asked, exchanging looks with him and laughing. My brother patted me on the head and gave me chocolates shaped like elephants and bears that he'd brought.

That April, I was admitted to the local primary school. Huge sycamore trees grew tall on either side of the school gate.

At the admissions interview, the teacher smiled and asked: "How many brothers and sisters do you have?"

I couldn't answer right away. My father, who'd accompanied me, hurriedly said, "Four." Then I was allowed to join the school.

From my second day there, I refused to let my mother go with me. Even on the first day, many children had gone on their own. They would twirl the bags that held their *zori* sandals and call out in loud voices as they made their way to school. I felt a strange dread of their high-spiritedness. When my mother insisted on taking me as far as the school gates despite my refusal, I kicked the root of one of the huge sycamore trees in despair. I developed a habit of kicking the roots of those trees by the school gate whenever I wanted to give myself courage.

I started to frequent my elder sisters' house in a quiet residential part of town, on the pretext of letting them help me with my schoolwork. My sisters had rented a large house with an old-fashioned iron-riveted gate, on which they'd pinned a sign announcing Koto Classes.

I had two other sisters besides my second sister Mina. The surviving two both suffered a wretched congenital misfortune; both were visually impaired from birth, their eyeballs entirely covered with a grayish film. They said that if they wore tinted glasses, they could dimly make out the expressions on people's faces. But being able to see things only dimly may actually have been harder to bear than being blind altogether. In their attempt to see things more clearly, they developed a habit of shaking their faces very delicately from side to side. That seemed a sad mannerism, even to me. Whenever I saw them approaching from the far end of the street, I would feel a lump in my throat and stand rooted to the spot. Wearing their matching tinted glasses, they would be walking hand in hand as they slowly crept along the edge of the road.

My eldest sister Aya was a qualified koto player from the Ikuta school. My third sister Kayo, though lacking qualifications, was by no means inferior in virtuosity. A total of about thirty female pupils would come in and out for lessons every day, and the overly large house echoed with the sound of koto music from morning to night. As long as the sound of the koto could be heard, the house was filled with a magical brilliance. There was not even the remotest hint of the dark shadows that accompanied the misfortune of my sisters.

My sisters didn't force me to study. Instead, they told me endless stories, both foreign fairy tales and Japanese folklore. To me, their stories were several times more enjoyable than my schoolwork—so much so that I would forget to go home and would wait instead for my sisters to finish their lessons. I found it quite astonishing that, even with their impaired vision, they could pluck the thirteen delicate strings of the koto without ever making a mistake. It seemed almost miraculous. When my sisters weren't there, I might secretly sit at the koto and imitate the posture I'd seen them adopt when playing. But when I shut my eyes, I had no idea even where the strings were, the plectrum would miss the mark completely, and the only sound I could make was painful to the ears.

My sister Aya had but one male companion. He was a poet called Sasa Tansui.

Sasa would often have long poems published in the local newspaper. The son of a distinguished samurai family, he had squandered his fortune on a local café waitress and, it was rumored, had been barred from his own home. Tall of stature, he would always wear an informal kimono, his head covered with a crumpled soft hat pulled so low over his brow that his eyes were hardly visible. His shins protruded like sticks beneath the hem of his kimono, and he wore felt sandals on his feet. He knew Aya to be a fond reader of a literary magazine called *Reijokai*, in which her submissions were occasionally published, and that was apparently why he first came visiting. After that, he started turning up unexpectedly, even when he had no particular business.

Aya valued Sasa Tansui, her only male friend. But Kayo and her pupils were afraid of him and called him Satan. If one of them saw him coming through the gate, she would cry, "It's Satan," and the others would all catch their breath.

Sometimes, though, Sasa was already standing unnoticed in the front garden before anyone knew it. The childlike pupils would then scream and huddle around my sisters. I wasn't particularly scared myself, as I considered him to be merely weird, and would watch the curious encounters between Aya and Satan without leaving my position on the edge of the verandah.

Satan usually arrived at dusk. The manner in which his lean, spindly figure would pass through the faint yellowish light, apparently floating among the potted plants as he approached, made it seem as though he were dispersing some sinister ghostly air as he walked. Without announcing himself at the front door, Satan would immediately go around to the garden and stand under the silk tree, from which reddish-pink blossoms cascaded down. Then, as if to give himself courage, he would slice the air two or three times with his whiplike bamboo walking stick and vigorously clear his throat. That must have been a call to Aya, for my sister would then appear on the verandah and kneel, blushing slightly, whereupon he would approach her with quickening steps, take a thick book with a black cover from his inside pocket and hand it to my sister without a word. She would remove a letter that had been slipped inside the title page, tilt it toward the failing light, and read it with her nose virtually pressed against it, then would bow deeply and withdraw to the study at the back. In the study were bookshelves crammed full with my sister's collection of books.

Satan would incessantly poke his stick at the ant traps that had been set out under the verandah, looking down all the while, until my sister came back out of the study clutching two or three books in her arms. On receiving the books, he would lift them up and bow in thanks—still with hat on head—before slipping them into his inside pocket. He would edge slowly backward until he reached the foot of the silk tree, the sides of his mouth turned down to form deep wrinkles on either side of his nose. Then he would suddenly disappear from our sight with a fleetness of foot that was quite in contrast to the fashion of his arrival.

My sister would squat at the edge of the verandah and look out toward the gate with eyes that could hardly see a thing.

That autumn was marked by a series of unhappy events.

At the beginning of autumn, Aya suddenly died.

Three days before her death, she fell into a deep sleep and would not wake even when called, causing a commotion inside our house. She continued to sleep soundly for the next three days, and in the end failed to wake up at all.

The day after she died, drizzle fell from dawn to dusk. Porters wearing livery that bore our shop's name lifted my sister's coffin onto their shoulders and carried it out through the gate. Outside the gate, a hearse was waiting.

All of a sudden a black police car pulled up, and just as it stopped in front of us, a policeman stepped out with a rattle of his saber.

"You there! Stop moving that coffin," he called loudly, his hand raised. Two other policemen and a man in a white coat also got out after him. The four of them surrounded my parents and began to argue. Eventually my father gritted his teeth and said, "I tell you, it's already been done. We're going to the crematorium now."

"You're not to put the coffin in there. Remove it now," one of the policemen said arrogantly.

Aya's coffin was once again hoisted onto the porters' shoulders and returned to the drawing room of the house. The family carpenter Kasuke wielded a large crowbar to pry open the lid in front of the police officers. A creaking, squeaking sound resonated loudly around the room, which was closed behind sliding doors. My mother covered both ears with her hands and closed her eyes.

When the lid had been fully removed, the man in the white coat, with a stethoscope around his neck, unceremoniously put his hand inside the coffin and started to probe dead Aya's face. He felt her eyes, then whispered to one of the policemen who stood watching self-importantly, felt her lips then whispered to the policeman again.

"Do you have to paw her like that? Do you have to abuse her like that even after she's dead?" my mother said from afar, as if she could take it no more.

The self-important policeman turned to her. "Quiet please," he said. "There are things the police need to do. We wish to examine her a little longer."

My mother ran out onto the verandah. I followed her there and suddenly saw Satan standing disconsolately in the rain, unnoticed under the silk tree in the garden, his shoulders slouched like a criminal.

In the middle of the autumn, my friend Orin died.

Orin had a chest ailment and hadn't been seen since the summer. Then she passed away without even waiting for her nose to fall off. The peach-colored neckpiece that I was supposed to give her still hung in our shop window for a little while after that. But one day a stranger with a crew cut came, said, "Could you lightly wrap that handtowel," bought it, and left.

Senta absconded at around the same time.

Senta was one of the apprentices who had been working in our shop with Goro since that spring. He was so cowardly that he would pale at the sight of a rat in broad daylight. One day, he went to collect our customers' payments and failed to return. My father refused to see Senta as a person who would do any wrong, and thinking that he may simply have gone home, sent Goro to check it out. I went with Goro to the old town district.

Just as my father had expected, we found Senta at the back of his tenement, near where a river flowed by a crumbling stone wall. Senta was crouched under a willow tree on the riverbank, gazing at a gamecock caged inside some wire netting. "Senta!" I called from behind, whereupon he leaped up in surprise and tried to escape along the riverbank. When he saw Goro standing there, he stopped in surprise again and suddenly jumped down into the river. The shallow water came up only to his knees.

"Hey, Senta!" Goro called sternly from the riverbank. "You went and stole the money, didn't you!"

"I did not! None of them would pay me!" Senta replied with a dismissive wave.

"Why didn't you go back to the shop, then?"

"Are you kidding? They poison themselves in there! The whole place scares me to death! Go on, get out of here, leave me alone!" Senta said as he started to walk back against the flow, splashing up sprays of water as he went.

Goro walked along the riverbank in step with him. "Don't be an idiot. It wasn't poison, I tell you! Come on out of there!" he said, raising his voice to persuade his friend.

But Senta just kept on walking up the river. "I'm never goin' back there again," he said tearfully. "Leave me alone! Leave me alone!"

Until I was eleven, I had to use the women's half of the public bath.

As evening closed in, my mother and I would duck under the perfume-scented curtain at the entrance to the women's baths, my dark-blue patterned kimono fastened with a dark brown obi. She would wash me, then take her time to carefully wash her own hair. While I waited, I would perch on the edge of the bathtub and look around absentmindedly. At such times, I would often see Orin's stepmother sitting with her bottom lodged on the tiled floor of the washing area while she busily washed her neck.

Her belly would repeatedly swell up then contract again. When it was contracted, the skin would hang down loosely, and milk from her dark nipples would trickle down onto it. When she saw me, she would break into a smile and show me her monkey-like baby wrapped in a towel.

"Look, I've had a baby boy. Do you want to play with him when he's older?" she would say in her Kyoto dialect. When she used Kyoto dialect, it meant she was in a good mood. She would use different dialects from different parts of the country, depending on her mood at the time. Then her belly would start to swell up again. When swollen to its limit it would glisten, like the belly of a celluloid kewpie doll, in the light of the setting sun that shone in through the window. Standing out prominently in the middle of her belly was a dark vertical line. For no particular reason, seeing that always reminded me of my dead friend Orin.

But then, why did Orin's stepmother always hate me when her belly was swollen to its limit? Heaving breath with her shoulders, she would constantly seem irritated. If I was perched on the edge of the bathtub, she would stare at me with cold eyes. "Move," she would say, almost pushing me off with the point of her protruding belly.

One day, I tried to lower myself into the bathtub alone while my mother was washing her hair. Orin's stepmother was loudly engaged in conversation with the other women as she splashed hot water onto her swollen belly. "Look, boy, you've got soap all over your neck. Go wash it off first!" she said, as if to make fun of me. As I turned my back on the women in embarrassment and slowly started to climb out, I could hear them talking quietly behind me.

"Whose boy is that?"

"You know," said Orin's stepmother, and went on to mention our shop by name. "His mother used to be called the 'local belle' or something. Well, she may have led a charmed life when she was younger, but look at her now!"

"Local belle? Yuck!" I said as if to myself, as I squatted next to my mother and rinsed the soap off my neck. She seemed not to have heard anything. Kneeling with her legs arranged neatly in front of her, she let her long hair flop down onto her thighs and rubbed it vigorously between her palms.

I also went to the baths with Shima, who was six years older than me.

Shima worked in our house as a maid. She was rather plump and had white skin. Her cheeks looked like someone had pasted red paper circles on them.

I liked Shima. After Orin died, I wanted to make Shima my wife. If a boy admitted to liking a girl called Yae-chan, the adults in my hometown would say, "Oh, really? Then you'll have to marry Yae-chan when you grow up!" I thought that liking someone was the same as marrying them.

After I'd started going to the baths with Shima, I began to notice a smell that was characteristic of the women's section. It would cause an odd tickling sensation at the back of my nose, which made it impossible for me to keep still. I would move my neck unnecessarily or thrust my arms out, or else shake nervously, much to Shima's annoyance when she was trying to wash me. Her cheeks would grow even redder and she would blink nervously as she tried to control me, but when my unruliness became too much for her, she would pull a stern face and grip my arms tightly in silence. As a reflex action, I would hit Shima around her thighs with my fists. Shima's velvety skin was full of elasticity, like a rubber doll. I was confused by the sensation of my rebounding fists.

When I was dressed again, I would duck under the wicket gate in front of the attendant's booth and sit cross-legged beside the boiler of the men's bath. There I would drink down a cupful of heavily salted barley water before manfully striding out of the bathhouse.

When I moved up to the fourth year, my school gave me a beautiful silver badge to pin on the breast of my jacket. It showed the school's initials in gold, surrounded by a cherry blossom. I gave Shima the old bronze badge that I had used until then. At first she hesitated, but when I took the silver badge in its paulownia box from my pocket and showed it to her, she was startled, immediately grabbed the bronze badge from the palm of my hand, and dropped it into her apron pocket.

The silver badge went well with my dark blue winter uniform but didn't look so good against the dappled pattern of the summer suit. When it was time for the seasonal change of clothes, Shima, with a knowing look, cut a little circle from a scrap of black cloth, sewed the badge on top of it, and fastened it to my dappled summer jacket with a safety pin. Now I walked to school with a swagger.

We were cleaning the classroom after school one summer day. The blacksmith's son was wearing new canvas shoes, and I accidentally splashed water from the floor mop onto one of them. I apologized, but he was utterly incensed.

"I only bought them at the market last night!" he screamed, and without further ado took the wet shoe off and hurled it to the ground. Astonishingly, the shoe bounced back up and landed smack on the edge of the cesspit, then mysteriously disappeared from sight. The blacksmith's son turned pale.

Taken aback by this turn of events, I peered into the cesspit in the hope of retrieving his shoe.

"Hey! Don't touch that!" he howled like a madman, thrusting his index finger at my chest as if pointing a gun at me. Then he started ranting about something entirely unrelated to his canvas shoes.

"Think you're dandy, don't you! Swishing around with your crappy bit of black cloth!"

I was caught unawares by the shock of what he'd said. The shame of his insult was so great that I lost my temper altogether.

"What?! I'll smash your stupid lumpy head in!" I yelled. In the middle of his forehead were blackish-blue lumps that refused to go away, and that was the one taunt he simply could not bear. He screwed his face up in a scowl and fell silent for a moment.

"What about your sister?" he suddenly started again. "She jumped off a boat into the sea! Glug glug glug!"

The spit flew from his mouth and landed at my feet. He continued to spray spit around as he flailed his arms in the air, imitating a person drowning. Our schoolmates, standing around us, started to get excited, which gave him courage to step up his attack.

"Your sister was eaten by a dolphin, your sister was eaten by a dolphin! Glug glug glug, glug glug glug!"

His eyes were brimming with tears of excitement. I couldn't understand what he meant, but his words immediately overwhelmed me. Filled with an unspeakable fear, I threw myself at him, simply to shut him up. He slumped feebly to the ground, then curled his body up like a shrimp. "Ask your mother if you don't believe me!" he said tearfully from under the arms that protected his head. "You're the only one who doesn't know! You should be ashamed of yourself."

The strength suddenly drained from my body and I looked down at him without a word. I wanted to cry, though I wasn't sad in the slightest. I hid my eyes with my arm but the tears welled up of their own volition.

I went home and stood vacantly behind Shima, who was squatting in front of the stove and lighting the fire for dinner.

"Ah, this smoke . . ." Shima said, turning away to see me standing there. I put my mouth to her ear.

"You know Mina, the one who died?" I asked quickly.

"Yes?"

"Do you know how she died?"

"How would I know that?" Shima shook her head vigorously and turned her face back down to the stove.

"She fell into the sea and drowned."

"Of course she didn't . . ." Shima said as if to scold me, but when I saw her stern eyes start to shift uncertainly, I instinctively felt that the blacksmith's son had been right.

I didn't want to believe it. I would happily have carried on without knowing it if I possibly could have. But at the same time I couldn't resist the temptation to peer into a secret that was about to give way. About a month later, I found a slim magazine in a drawer of my mother's dresser. It was a local poetry journal called *Hanakago*. My mother had no interest in composing poems. Recalling the words of the old man in the formal kimono at my sister Mina's funeral, I started to feel uneasy. I quickly rolled up the magazine and took it upstairs, where I would be alone. I felt too scared to start from the beginning, so I turned to the back page. There, I immediately saw my sister's name with a black box around it. Under that was an article lamenting my sister's suicide. Apparently she had been one of the editors of the magazine. One month before I'd started school, it seemed that my middle sister Mina had thrown herself from a ferryboat into the northern sea straits, where schools of dolphins were known to live.

I felt unbearably ashamed on learning this. Rather than wanting to know Mina's reasons for killing herself, I was filled with a sense of shame at her suicide. I stood alone forlornly in the altar room. I looked up at Mina's photograph. She was smiling, her chin doubled inside her neatly arranged collar. My sister, the owner of this beautiful smiling face, plummeted into the white foam of the sea from the deck of a ship, then bobbed up and down amid a school of dolphins. When I imagined the scene, I felt my cheeks starting to flush of their own accord.

It was around this time that I noticed the repulsiveness of my appearance.

One day, I went to the barber's with a firm resolve. I wanted to get a close-cropped haircut, instead of the German cut I'd always had.

The "German cut" was a boy's hairstyle in which the back was trimmed short but the bangs were grown long. In the town where I was born, this was the preferred hairstyle of boys from respectable and well-to-do families. It was the driver of the horse-dray that passed through the town's main street who was most sensitive to the difference in children's hairstyles. If he noticed a boy with a German cut hanging from the back of his wagon, he would stop his horse and say, "Hello there? You shouldn't do that, it's dangerous, you know!"

But if he found a boy with cropped hair messing about with his wagon, he would deliberately hurry the horse along and swirl the ends of his reins like a lasso. "Little brat! Come on, then, if you want to be trampled to death!" he would roar while giving a ferocious glare.

Aspiring to become one of those brats, I ignored my regular barber and went to another some distance away. That was when I caught sight of my bizarre appearance in the barber's distorted mirror.

My face should have been circular in outline with well-rounded cheeks, but now looked horribly angular with high cheek bones and a sharp, pointed chin. My eyes had an unpleasantly reddish glimmer that startled even me. The back of my exposed head was surprisingly long. Not only that, but it also had a round indentation in it, as if a bowl had been placed over an ordinary head. The barber's clipper raced smoothly up my head after cutting my fringe, then made a large dipping motion as it went over the indentation.

The willfulness of my behavior amazed all who knew me and saddened my mother. It wasn't the cropped hair that saddened her so much as the fact that I'd acted impulsively, without telling her. My father stared at my head dubiously, then averted his eyes without saying a word.

When I exposed my long head to the gaze of others, I felt indescribably desolate, as if I were receiving some kind of punishment, as well as a sense of relief at no longer being a child. Then again, I was depressed, as I felt this punishment to be unjust, one that I had not earned. I was so utterly dejected that Shima grew suspicious and asked the reason. I answered that I was embarrassed about my head being so long. Shima laughed nonchalantly.

"Don't be silly!" she said. "Ryu at Kinboshi has got a far longer head, hasn't he? You have nothing to worry about, at all."

Kinboshi was a seedy bar in a back street near our house. I was forbidden to go to such places, but at that moment I suddenly wanted to go there precisely because it was forbidden. I crept along under the eaves of the houses, then slipped into the back street and ducked under the rope curtain at Kinboshi's door. Ryu and I laughed weakly at each other across a table upon which earthen saké bottles lay on their sides.

I became a frequent visitor at Kinboshi.

Ryu and I would play several quick games of *shogi* under the lucky cat statue that stood, blackened with soot, in a corner of the gloomy bar. The bar was always filled with a thick, heavy sultriness, mixed with the smell of soy sauce, cooking oil, and saké. Kinboshi's customers were ditchdiggers, horse drivers, mendicant priests, rickshaw men, traveling performers, street peddlers. The sight of them sitting around in a circle and drumming on the sides of their rice bowls as they sang out of tune captivated my heart. Thinking how saddened my mother would be if she could see me immersed in such seediness, I felt my mind strangely put at ease by the sensation of doing something that I shouldn't have been.

Before I knew it, the curious melody of the song sung by Kinboshi's customers had become etched upon my mind. When I got home, I sang it to Shima. She listened until the end, although she looked a little annoyed. "You're not to sing that song," she said at length. "You're a bad boy. I'm not to blame."

I'm not to blame either, I thought to myself.

In the autumn of the year before I left primary school, Shima abandoned me. She had to return to her home in the countryside because she was going to get married.

When I heard about this from my mother, I wanted to laugh. I felt as if Shima had deceived us all. I was lying next to her in the maid's room as she busied herself with some needlework.

"Shima," I said. "Is it true you're going away to the country to get married?"

"What? You think I'm going to ride off on a horse or some-thing, without any wedding dress? Certainly not!"

Shima glanced at me and giggled. For some reason I also found it funny, and rolled around the tatami floor laughing.

But Shima deceived me in the end.

One morning, she crouched on the ground in front of me as I peered into the goldfish bowl on the verandah, and said goodbye to me with a stony expression. She asked me not to go to places like Kinboshi any more. I listened vacantly to her faltering voice, but when she looked away and went to stand up, I flew at her without a word. With the tips of my fingers I sharply pinched her red cheeks, which seemed a little paler than usual.

"You're going then?"

"Yes. They've come to collect me. I've got to go now."

Her voice already sounded like the voice of a stranger—and not only because she was tensing her cheeks.

I was utterly disconsolate. Why did all the people who were closest to me always have to abandon me like this? After Shima had gone back to the maid's room, I could bear it no longer and clambered up the steep roof on the main part of the house. The top of the roof offered a panoramic view of the yellow fields in the far distance. Beyond the fields flowed a gentle line of dull brown mountains. Shima was going back to her home at the foot of those mountains.

The stagecoach sounded its horn as it passed in front of our house. I could see Shima running toward the coach with a man I didn't know. Shima was wearing a dark-blue kimono with white splash patterns and a red obi. When she disappeared into the carriage, led by the hand of the unknown man, I caught a glimpse of her white calves. Sitting astride the ridge-end tile and watching as clouds of dust were blown up by the departing stagecoach, I spat repeatedly in all directions.

The following year, I moved up to a secondary school on the outskirts of town.

One day at the end of the first month of school, the class teacher summoned me and asked me to find out the current addresses of my two eldest brothers. They were both old boys of the school. I went home and duly reported this to my father. "Really," he said with a frown. At that moment, I thought I saw an expression of terrible discomfort pass over his face.

The following morning, my father gave me a sealed letter, along with my second brother's address. He'd written all about my eldest brother in the letter and I should just hand it over to the teacher, my father said in a gentle voice, with his eyelids blinking hard. I put the letter in the inside pocket of my jacket and left for school, but as I walked along I started to experience a stifling feeling caused by a certain misgiving.

I started wondering where my eldest brother could be now. I hadn't seen anything of him for a long time. My family had stopped talking about him altogether. Was he dead? If so, I certainly had no memory of a funeral. Come to think of it, I knew that his photograph had been neatly removed from our family album. Why was that? I felt a foreboding.

I followed my usual route and entered a broad field. Every morning, I would avoid the town and walk to school through the fields. That morning the sunlight was dazzlingly bright. The smoke of a bonfire drifted faintly, hazily over the field. I walked slowly with the ungainly step of one who is about to do wrong. As I walked on, I took the letter from my pocket and opened the envelope. The letter was written in brush and ink on rolled writing paper.

Dear Sirs:

Concerning your inquiry after my eldest son Fumiya: to tell the honest truth, he disappeared eight years ago and has not been seen since. He is missing at the time of this writing. I once heard a rumor that he was living in Kyoto, but cannot be sure of this. The times being what they are, my search for him is not going well . . .

I lacked the energy to read on to the end. The only thing that remained clear was a sensation of falling—one more person had left me. I felt slightly dizzy as I folded the letter back into the envelope, then squatted at the edge of a stream and cast the screwed-up envelope into its flow, watching vacantly as it slid along the surface of the water.

On my way home from school that day, I bought a tourist map from the station shop. I was going to search for my eldest brother. In my memory he was nothing but a figure of fear. It was he who had struck me on the head with his chopstick holder. But now I badly wanted to meet him. I wanted to meet him and bring him home with me. I feared that if I didn't, the bond of kinship between us would loosen and unravel altogether.

I could no longer look my remaining family members full in the face. Whatever the circumstances behind my brother's disappearance, I couldn't understand why he should be so neglected when he may be alive. To be sure, the strange cheerfulness that pervaded our house was also a mystery to me. The unnatural deaths of my sisters, my brother's disappearance—yet in spite of it all, everyone in my family smiled cheerfully at each other as if nothing had happened. I felt a certain distrust of them. Even if their sorrow was so deep that their only way of surviving was simply to look at each other and smile, this was something that I could not comprehend at the time.

I came to a simple decision. I would go on a journey.

After going to bed that night, I opened up the map by my pillow. Japan was a surprisingly large country. The white expanse of its long, narrow landmass was criss-crossed with a bewildering network of railways that resembled lines on the palm of a hand.

Kyoto. I looked for Kyoto. First I would go to Kyoto. Even if it was only a rumor, there was nowhere else to start looking. Kyoto was more than seven hundred miles from my hometown. And within Kyoto were Nakagyo Ward, Fushimi Ward, Higashiyama Ward. In my sense of helplessness at the prospect of wandering this unknown land, the map became so hazy at times that I could barely see it at all.

I lacked the essential traveling expenses. The only person I could consider asking for money was my father, but he had kept the truth about my brother and sisters entirely secret until now. Even if I could lie about the purpose of my trip, my parents would never permit me to go on such a journey alone as a twelve-year-old. I thought of my second brother. He was a *brother*, after all; he would understand. If I explained it to him, perhaps he would tell me what to do. I felt him now the only person I could turn to.

For the first time in my life, I wrote a long letter to one of my brothers. It was the hardest piece of work I had ever done until then. My brother's reply arrived by return post.

Don't be a fool. This is none of your business—I'll tell you about it when you're older. You would do better to concentrate on correcting your unmanly ways.

The letter was accompanied by a heavy parcel.
I opened the parcel. It was a set of *kendo* fencing gear.

And All Promenade!

IT WAS MY WIFE Fusako who found the apartment. She called me at work to tell me about it right away.

"I found one!" she said, her voice dancing with barely concealed elation. "It's in a really nice area. It's just been built, and none of the apartments are occupied yet. Each has two rooms and a kitchen of its own! The rent is fifty-five hundred yen. And there's no key money or deposit to pay! What do you think?"

Two rooms for fifty-five hundred yen—it didn't sound bad at all. I was rather surprised. I knew that my wife had been looking here and there during her daily walks with our daughter Momoe, who'd only just discovered the joy of walking. But I could never have imagined that she would happen upon such a rare bargain.

"Well, that sounds good," I said. "We'd better put down an advance quickly."

"Yes," she replied, and started giggling.

"What is it?"

"Actually, I've already paid the advance."

That day, I left work at five o'clock and hurried straight back to the room we were renting in the suburbs. We had already been given notice that we would need to leave. It had been all right while our old landlady was living on her own, but when her youngest daughter, who'd previously left home, returned with a younger man in tow, we were suddenly too much for her. Still, the prospect suited us as well. We'd originally rented the room as a stopgap, when I first came up from the country alone to take up my present occupation. Lacking the resources to move out, I'd later called Fusako to join me there. But when our child started to stand, then walk, then run around on her own, the room became far too cramped. We were starting to think that we'd have to move to a larger place soon, but were still procrastinating when the landlady gave us notice to leave.

By the time I returned home, my wife had spread out all our belongings over the floor of our tiny room and was making preparations for the move. Our daughter, deprived now of a place to play, sat plopped on the middle shelf of the built-in closet, where she was laughing gaily at something that amused her.

"Sorry it's such a mess," said Fusako as she came to welcome me in.

"Don't put her up there," I said. "She could fall." I walked over to the closet and lifted the child into my arms.

I couldn't help feeling that my wife had become slack in her supervision of Momoe since the child had started to walk. Fusako seemed capable of handling her with great confidence, probably out of some kind of maternal instinct. But looking on from the outside, her style sometimes seemed dangerous and difficult to watch. I just wished she would be more careful. The slightest slip in concentration, and our daughter's life could have been ruined.

"Well, if we're moving anyway, it can't come soon enough!" said my wife.

"When shall we go?"

"The sooner the better. Tomorrow, if you like."

In the end, we decided to go and see the new apartment together, and quickly ate our dinner.

"I found it when I wasn't even looking," said Fusako as she carried food with her chopsticks now to her own mouth, now to Momoe's. She began to relate how she had happened upon the apartment.

That morning, she had tired herself out doing the laundry. She had decided not to go looking for apartments that day, but instead to go shopping at the station market three stops away on the suburban railway line. When she'd finished the shopping she felt hungry, and asked Momoe what she would like to eat. "Udon!" the child had answered. So the pair of them had gone into a noodle restaurant near the market, and had ordered two bowls of udon soup noodles with fried tofu.

The restaurant wasn't particularly busy, but their udon took an unusually long time to appear. Fusako turned repeatedly toward the serving window to see what was taking so long. Through the window she could see steam billowing up in the kitchen. Then she suddenly noticed, on the wall above the serving window, a

small handwritten sign with the words NEWLY BUILT APART-
MENTS written at the top. Of course, she must have noticed it
there before. But until then she'd assumed it was an advertise-
ment for a specialty seasonal dish or something, and had made
no attempt to read it. Her curiosity aroused, she got up and went
to read the sign. 4½-MAT & 3-MAT ROOMS, OWN KITCHEN, NO
KEY MONEY/DEPOSIT, 5,500 YEN/MONTH, SUNNY, CHILDREN
WELCOME, it read.

In her surprise, Fusako immediately called through the serving window.

"Excuse me, do these apartments belong to an estate agent?"

A man who appeared to be the proprietor pushed his head
through.

"No, the apartment owner asked us to put the sign up. We
only put it there this morning," he said. "No one's asked about
them yet, so you should be all right if you go over there now."
And he carefully explained how to get to the apartments.

"Funny, isn't it," my wife concluded. "You look everywhere
with no luck, then suddenly you get what you want when you
least expect it."

"Things happen like that when your luck's in," I said.

"I suppose so. It's funny. If Momoe had said she wanted something else—ice cream, say—it wouldn't have happened at all." A
pensive expression came over her face. "It's such a thin line that
separates good luck from bad, huh."

"Everything's luck. It's a very thin line," I said. Fusako continued to share food with Momoe in silence.

"It's frightening," she suddenly said after a few moments.

As soon as we'd finished eating, we went to see the new apartment, the three of us holding hands, with Momoe in the middle.

We took the outbound train and got off three stops along the line. We walked for about ten minutes from the station along a broad asphalt road that ran on either side of the tracks. The apartments were in an area dotted sparsely with homes. *Apartments* was perhaps not the word—they were little more than rear tenements, with four rooms lined up behind a little confectionery shop that faced onto the main road. The owner of the confectionery shop was the landlord. Fusako went into the shop, and the owner eventually appeared, accompanied by a young woman with a bad leg. She was his wife.

"Good evening," she said courteously. "This way, please."

From a little path beside the house, she opened a glass door at the entrance and went in. Inside, she shone a flashlight down a long, narrow concrete corridor. On one side were a scullery and a toilet. On the other, four doors stood in a line with windows separating them.

"There are four apartments, but they're all the same inside," the woman said. She showed us into the first one. Behind the plywood door was a small square entrance measuring about three by three feet with a concrete floor, and beyond that, unpartitioned, another small square room for the kitchen. The three-mat room was nearest to the corridor, while the four-and-a-half mat room faced the outside. There was a built-in closet in the larger room and a small storage closet in the smaller room. Both of the closets had plywood doors. There was nothing we could do about the front door, but I supposed we would have to cover the storage closets with decorative screen paper. The walls were pale blue. Sliding open the glass door and rain shutter in the larger room, I spied a small open verandah outside.

"Is there a garden out there?" I asked.

"No, just a passageway."

"A passageway?" I said bleakly.

"Yes. It leads to the house in back. A policeman lives there," the woman answered, as if anticipating my question.

While I looked around the apartment, Fusako remained standing in the tiny entrance. "Isn't this a big house?" she cooed to the child on her back. "It'll be your home soon. We're all going to move here tomorrow."

"Not bad, is it?" I said once we were back in the corridor.

"Really? I'm glad to hear that!" Fusako sounded very happy. Her mind was made up already.

"But you know, the kitchen does look cramped. It can't be bigger than a telephone booth!"

"That's true. But I can cope with that. We can't have everything we want. Besides, we don't have much in the way of kitchen things. And it'll be the first time I've had my own kitchen. It'll be just right."

"Okay. Well, that settles it, then."

We both wanted the apartment at the end of the corridor, but it was right in front of the toilet, so we decided to rent the one next to it. After all, as long as the three of us could live without feeling hemmed in or inhibited by others, anywhere would be fine.

We decided to move in the following day, and with that took our leave.

"Not having to pay key money or a deposit is unusual these days," I said to the woman in parting. "That's a big help."

"Well, my father not only built this house, but decided all those things as well. He's a hard-working man, not the greedy type," she laughed. These did seem like good people.

"Good night then," I said with that thought in mind.

"Good night."

It was my turn to carry Momoe on my back. We set off once more along the sparsely lit asphalt road.

Suddenly, we heard the woman's voice calling behind us.

"Er, excuse me!" she said. "Were you wanting to go home?"

"That's right," I answered.

The woman put her hand to her mouth and laughed.

"Well, you're going toward the river! The station's this way," she said, pointing in the opposite direction.

"Oh my goodness," Fusako said to me. "You silly thing."

"But you were walking this way!"

"I was not! I thought it was odd, but you seemed so confident that I just followed you!"

"What?!"

The woman continued to laugh as she went back indoors.

We turned and started retracing our steps.

"Well, that was close," said Fusako. "You have no sense of direction. Who knows where you'll lead us next?"

I assumed she was joking at my expense; her tone suggested

as much. Even so, I wondered whether perhaps she was using the joke to express an anxiety that she usually kept hidden deep inside. Whatever the case, her comment cut deeply, since there was more than an element of truth in it.

Let us have a good life, I prayed to myself. It was a prayer I'd repeated many times, many dozens of times in the past. For me, it was always a new prayer. *Let's make a new start and try to have a good life.*

As I adjusted the child's position on my back, I noticed that she'd fallen fast asleep.

It rained the next day, as luck would have it, but we still went ahead with our move.

The move went easily enough, of course, since we had few possessions. Bedding for two, a small chest of drawers, a sideboard, a small bureau, a low dining table, a small bookcase, and a few books from my student days that I couldn't bring myself to part with (though I'd long since lost the habit of reading)—these, and the pram we'd used for Momoe, were more or less our only belongings of note. We asked the local moving company to send a convertible three-wheeler truck in the morning, loaded everything into it and took it all over in one go. Once at the apartment, we unloaded the things into the four-mat room from the verandah. I left the tidying up to my wife, hitched a ride back on the truck, and raced to the station. Being an ordinary employee, I couldn't take time off work on a weekday just to move to a new house.

When I returned to the new apartment that evening, the

furniture had already been neatly laid out in the rooms. During the afternoon, the confectionery shop owner had come over with the rental agreement, and had helped Fusako rearrange our things while he was there. The chest and sideboard were lined up along the wall of the larger room, the bookcase and bureau beside the window in the smaller room, and the low dining table in the middle of the larger room, all in their rightful places in a proper homely setting.

As I closed the glass door, the smell of freshly planed wood wafted through.

"Ah! The smell of a new apartment!" I clasped my hands behind my back and started plodding around our new residence, tiny as it was.

"Don't do that!" said my wife. "You look like a detective on a house search! Take your raincoat off, at least."

I came to my senses and took off my coat, but didn't know where to put it.

"Where do we put our coats?" I asked her.

"Can't you find somewhere?" she replied, reluctant to leave the first kitchen she could call her own.

If she hadn't made a place for a coat rack, there surely wasn't one yet.

I took a hammer and some nails and went to put up some makeshift coat hooks in the smaller room. As I was looking for a suitable spot, I noticed that a nail was already protruding from the wall between the window and the entrance. At first I assumed that the carpenter must have put it there for some reason and forgotten to remove it. It angered me to think that the idiot had just left a nail sticking out from our wall. I decided to pull it out with the claw end of the hammer.

When I touched the wall with the hammer, it made a twanging noise—not a noise I would normally associate with a wall. This seemed odd, so I knocked the wall lightly with the hammer to make sure. *Twang twang.* I tapped it with the tip of my finger. *Twang twang.* I rubbed it with my finger. I could feel fine protrusions that felt like fibers. I brought my eye right up to the wall and looked at it closely. It was made of plywood.

My face was stiff with astonishment. I shouted to my wife, or so I intended. In fact, I already seemed to be restraining my voice in awareness of listening ears outside the apartment. Fusako emerged from the kitchen with a flustered expression.

"Take a look at this," I said, pointing at the wall.

"A cockroach?" she said with a frown.

"Come on, look at it closely!"

"You don't have to talk like that!"

I grabbed her hand with no great delicacy and placed her palm flat against the wall. She kept her eyes on me, but the expression on her face was the one she normally uses when taking our daughter's temperature. After a moment, she slowly turned her gaze to the wall. Then she brushed my hand away and withdrew her own hand from the wall.

"It's plywood, isn't it?" she said, eyeing me sternly.

"That's right," I replied.

My mind had already been overtaken by a strange calm that invariably descends on me when I encounter such situations. I suppose you could call it an undue lack of moral fiber. Whenever it happens, I find myself unable to feel anger, sadness, or even happiness in a straightforward way. It's a kind of passive courage that makes me want to accept everything without question, to resign myself to things that cannot be changed.

"We've been tricked, haven't we?" My wife's anger was straightforward.

"Not tricked. I'd just say we've been careless."

"What? They've deliberately made it look like a real wall!"

"Yes, but still, the woman's father has obviously tried his hardest, and perhaps this was the best he could do. Maybe he thinks he's done a good enough job. And anyway, no one has actually claimed that it's a real wall, have they?"

"How can you be so calm about it?" Fusako looked at me reproachfully. "Aren't you worried? Aren't you put out at all?"

"Yes, but there's nothing I can do about it."

She seemed about to explode, but it was clear that she was already restraining herself. She simply stared at me with a look of disbelief.

It wasn't that I didn't know how suffocating, how ruinous for the nerves the world of plywood could be, or how it could spoil the sensations of domestic life. At the same time, however, I also knew that anyone who strayed into the world of plywood would not be strong enough to extricate himself from it easily.

"Well, let's put up with it for the time being. At least a plywood wall won't move, so I suppose it's better than a paper screen."

At that moment, someone sneezed in the next apartment. But there was no one in the next apartment. When she realized that it was the landlord who was sneezing, in his own house three doors away, Fusako assumed a look of despair and started tapping all the walls of the apartment with the handle of her feather duster, as if to inspect them.

Twang twang, twang twang.

Seeing this, Momoe grew quite excited. "Me too, me too!" she shouted, and immediately started hitting any wall within reach with both hands.

Twang twang, twang twang.
Twang, twang, twang, twang.
And so started our life of happy harmony.

Within four or five days, the other three apartments were all occupied. The first to go was Number One, nearest the entrance, followed by Number Two, and finally the last along the corridor, Number Four, with ourselves at Number Three. Predictably, Number Four, the one that faced the toilet, was the last to be taken.

It was impossible to know whether the occupants had been aware of the plywood walls before they'd moved in, or whether they'd only discovered them later. If the latter, they would surely have noticed very quickly. The fact that none of them complained was probably because they, too, had resigned themselves to it. They all lived such terribly quiet lives; they must have been painfully aware, not only of the noise coming from beyond their walls, but also of the fact that any noise they themselves made could be readily heard on the other side. Surely they were all biting their tongues and suppressing their emotions.

Number Four was the only exception.

The occupant of apartment Number Four was a woman who

lived on her own. Hers was the kind of freewheeling lifestyle that could only be achieved by someone who'd been accustomed to living within plywood walls for some time.

The woman was about thirty years old, small in build, yet with a taut physique and a dark, leathery tan. I soon learned that her name was Emi, because she constantly referred to herself as such when talking to other residents in the scullery. In fact, talking seemed to be a favorite pastime of hers. She would rattle away in her harsh, gravelly voice whenever she succeeded in trapping another resident busy with laundry in the scullery. Since she often mentioned Yokohama and Tachikawa, I assumed she had lived there too at some time in the past.

Every Monday and Friday evening, this Emi was visited by the same man—a red-faced, middle-aged American who drove a battered cobalt-blue car. He would turn off the asphalt road into the passageway that led to the back and park right next to her verandah. "Hey, baby!" he would call out to Emi in his contrabass voice. "Hello!" she would reply in a nasal voice as she came out to meet him. And for the next few hours, the two of them would play jazz on the radio while merrily frolicking around the apartment, with the occasional shrieks or bursts of laughter. Then the man would climb back into his battered car and ride off again.

As soon as the man had left, however, Emi used to do something very strange. She would crouch at the foot of her bed and pray. I don't know what she was praying for, or to whom. But once Emi had seen the man off, she always prayed like that without fail.

When I first heard Emi praying, I thought she must have been crying. It seemed strange that something could have suddenly made her so sad when, only moments earlier, she'd been romping around so gaily. But after a few such occasions, I noticed that her voice, which sounded like a sob at first, would suddenly change to a tone of quiet recollection, or one of censure. Once the man had left, there could surely be no one else inside Emi's apartment. She must have been talking to herself.

My curiosity was aroused by this woman who could so openly cavort with the man while he was there, and then, when he had gone, appear to cry or talk to herself. Of course, I couldn't ask her about it directly. In any case, the following morning, she would amuse herself chattering in the scullery as usual, as though nothing had happened. She would prattle on endlessly, laugh raucously, or hum songs under her breath. She certainly didn't seem like a woman who would quietly indulge in such a private late-night performance.

It was a humid evening about a month after that first occasion. The man had already left Emi's apartment.

Every evening after dinner, I would pick up our daughter and take her outside for a walk while Fusako tidied the apartment and put the bedding out. That evening, I left the apartment block as usual and walked up and down the asphalt road in front of the landlord's shop. Then I returned to the apartments by the passageway that led to our verandah.

Glancing across at Number Four, I noticed that the rain shutter was open by about a foot. It always remained closed when the man was visiting, but this evening, for some reason, it was open. Perhaps it was because this particular evening was quite sultry, or perhaps because Emi had a habit of opening the shutter to change the musty air inside the apartment after the man had left.

I nonchalantly strolled past the apartment and casually glanced inside. There, at the partition between the two rooms, Emi was squatting with her back toward me. She seemed to be resting her forehead on the end of her Western-style double bed, which occupied the whole of the smaller room. At first sight, she looked as if she might be searching for something she had lost under the bed.

I walked on to the policeman's house at the end of the passageway, then turned back when a dog started barking at me. When I passed Emi's apartment again, she was still in the same position as before.

This seemed quite odd. Once back in our apartment, I could hear Emi's voice as usual. I asked my wife when it had started. She said it had started soon after I'd left. In other words, every evening, Emi must have been talking to herself while crouched in that position, as if reproaching someone.

It suddenly struck me that her pose appeared to be one of prayer. Perhaps Emi was praying toward the bottom of the bed at those times. Of course, I have no way of knowing what lay under the bed. But I thought there must be something hidden there, something that she felt compelled to pray to after the man had left. In a sense, that would have been the best place to hide something, whether from him or from anyone else.

From that time on, whenever I heard Emi praying, I would feel as though I'd been woken from my sleep, as if I was straining to listen in silence to my own inner self—and this had nothing to do with the plywood walls.

I don't know why that was so.

Every morning, I would leave our apartment just before eight, cross the asphalt road to the station, and take the suburban railway into the center of Tokyo. I worked in the dispatch section of a small transport company that handled mainly express deliveries by truck. I was in my third year with the company.

Before that, I worked in the operations department of a publisher that specialized in academic texts. I'd joined the company right after graduating from university, but had been there only a little more than a year when it suddenly folded. It was while I was there that I married Fusako. When the company folded, she was expecting our child. I had to stay on for a while to help resolve a few last issues for the company, but as I had no firm prospects of finding a new job, I planned to return to my family home in the country to think things over. I sent Fusako on ahead, then joined her there later. We stayed for about six months, during which time Fusako gave birth to Momoe. When my new job unexpectedly turned up, we did the same thing in reverse—I traveled to Tokyo first, my wife following on later with the baby.

My new job was neither particularly easy nor particularly difficult. It took some time to get used to the work, and I sometimes found it quite hard. But after a couple of years, I grew accustomed to it and soon no longer found it hard at all. I would, however, sometimes become irritated with the monotony of my daily work.

Even if the work wasn't difficult, my irritation prevented it from seeming easy.

I always left work at five and arrived back at the apartment just after six. Sometimes I might go for a drink on the way home with my bosses or workmates. Even then, I would always make my excuses by ten at the latest and take the suburban railway home.

My bosses and workmates used to poke fun at me for this, calling me a "doting husband." Well, if a man who hurries home to the nest is a doting husband, it can't be helped. My station was a long way down the line and the trains stopped running quite early in the evening. Whenever I inadvertently missed the last train I was really in a fix.

Once, forgetting that we'd moved, I missed the long-distance train and had to get out at the station two stops before our own. From there I walked home along the railway tracks in the dark. An old friend from university had invited me out, and we'd been on a crawl through the bars in the nightlife district.

My friend's name was Koike. I'd met him among a group of idlers who were somehow flung together during our student days, but since leaving university the two of us had drifted apart. Our "friendship" merely consisted of meeting up once a year or so, when one of our number came to Tokyo from the country, for example. One day, this Koike called me at work. He asked if we could get together that evening, as there was someone he wanted me to meet. When I asked who it was, he wouldn't give a name, but merely said that it was a woman.

My curiosity aroused, I agreed to meet him. Koike took me to a bar near a train station downtown. The bar was so small that it would have been full with only five customers. It was empty when we arrived, apart from a thin woman of around thirty-five or six who was sitting behind the counter reading a newspaper, her hair tied up in a bun.

When I saw the woman, I thought I'd seen her somewhere before, but couldn't quite remember where. When she saw me, however, she said "Hello there" as if she immediately remembered, and called me by name. Seeing my look of surprise, Koike laughed in evident amusement. "Well?" he said. "Shall I tell you?" But before he could say anymore, it came back to me. What jogged my memory was her habit of blinking incessantly when she felt self-conscious. That, and the dark freckles that spread from her nose under her eyes.

The woman had lived with one of our friends, Higuchi, for just over a year during our student days, before he cast her aside. We had graduated five years earlier, and this had happened in our third year at university, so exactly seven years had passed. I must have seen her several times back then, when I was with Higuchi. I remembered that she had been seven years older than Higuchi. She had aged significantly and was now quite haggard-looking. Back then, she had worked in a department store and always dressed stylishly.

"Oh, it's you!" I said, surprised in so many ways. I had forgotten her name.

"After all these years! What a nice surprise," she said. Still smiling bashfully, she started to pour saké from a large bottle into a smaller ceramic bottle for serving. As she poured, large round tears began to roll down her cheeks in rapid succession. Then, as suddenly as they had appeared, they stopped. The woman continued to pour the saké as if nothing had happened, without even breaking her smile. She made no attempt to wipe her eyes; in fact, they didn't even look wet.

Actually, it seemed an agreeable way of crying. There are some who can lie down and start snoring in an instant, then arise as soon as they're woken. They are known as "good sleepers." In the same way, this woman could have been called a good crier. It wasn't something that anyone could have imitated.

She must have had it pretty hard since Higuchi left her, I thought.

On the one hand, I didn't want to stay at all. But I couldn't just leave, as if I'd merely gone there to poke fun at her. So I lingered indecisively. While we were there, she didn't once mention Higuchi. And we took care to avoid all subjects that were in any way linked to him, confining ourselves to small talk instead.

It was already late when I parted from Koike and headed for the train station. I carelessly slipped into my old routine, forgetting that we had moved from our previous apartment. Two stops short of my station, there was an announcement to say that the service was terminating there. To make matters worse, the connecting local train had already finished for the night. I had no alternative but to walk home along the railway tracks, which cut through the fields and provided the shortest route home. Besides, I was unlikely to lose my way if I followed the tracks.

It was a clear, though moonless, night, and the wooden

railroad ties glowed a pale shade of white in the starlight. As I stepped from one tie to the next, I suddenly thought again of the woman's tears, and how unusually large they had been. Now, so many years later, she could cry as simply as that, and yet still not make one mention of the past. In the old days, she must have cried a great deal.

I don't know how she and Higuchi had met and become romantically attached, but before I knew it, the pair of them were living together in his apartment. Whenever I went there, Higuchi would act the overbearing husband and simply do as he pleased. She, on the other hand, would always smile in resignation, like an older sister embarrassed by the wild antics of her younger brother. In spite of this, they seemed a perfectly harmonious couple, from the outside.

When exactly a year had passed, Higuchi one day invited Koike and me to their apartment, saying it was their "anniversary." On our arrival, we saw that Higuchi's girlfriend had also invited three friends. Two of them were coworkers from the department store, and the other a childhood friend from her hometown. The friend was a primary school teacher who had come to Tokyo to attend a summer course. As I recall, the teacher was a real beauty, with rounded cheeks and bright eyes.

That night we all ate and drank ourselves silly, missed our trains, and ended up spending the night on the floor. There were two rooms, one with six tatami mats, and the other with three. Since they were a couple, Higuchi and his girlfriend slept in the smaller room, while the five guests occupied the larger one. It was a muggy night in August, and we didn't need much in the way of bedding, so Koike and I spread out a blanket and slept on top of it.

I awoke early the next morning with a terrible hangover, and went out to the kitchen for a drink of water. The others were still asleep, but Higuchi also got up and followed me in. "I did it!" he said, bringing his mouth in close to my ear.

"Did what?" I asked, looking him in the face.

"I did it with the teacher!" he replied with a roguish grin.

"When?"

"Last night."

"Liar," I said, laughing.

"It's true!"

"How could you do it with everyone lying on the floor around you?" I asked. He chuckled but gave no reply.

"How did it happen?"

"I don't know! It just happened."

"What if your girlfriend had noticed?"

"I'll deal with that when the time comes! Anyway, whether she noticed or not, she slept the whole night facing the chest of drawers."

I stared at him, appalled.

It was about a week later that Higuchi and his girlfriend broke up. I don't know whether she knew about his infidelity that night, but in any case, his interest in the schoolteacher finished their relationship. I don't even know if he or the schoolteacher had initiated it. But for about three days before they separated, the girlfriend was said to have cried whenever she spoke, as if she was incapable of saying anything without weeping.

Following the separation, Higuchi apparently met the teacher a few times, but only during that summer. It all ended when she returned to her school in the countryside. After that, Higuchi went back to his hometown, where he married and became the town's youngest-ever representative to the local council.

I have no idea what path led his old girlfriend to that downtown bar.

But their relationship had been nothing more than a whimsical fling.

After walking for a while, I suddenly noticed that the sound of my footsteps on the railroad ties had changed. They had been making a crisp, hard noise, but now the sound had grown dull and reverberant. Thinking this strange, I looked down at my feet. I noticed that the ground beneath the railroad ties had been replaced by water, its dark surface reflecting the starlit sky.

Without realizing it, I had wandered onto a railway bridge that crossed a river. If I hadn't noticed, I would have just walked right over. I stopped walking immediately and stood rooted to a single railroad tie, my legs as rigid as posts.

Please forgive me.

That was how my wife started her letter. It arrived while I was still in Tokyo winding up the business of the collapsed publishing company. Fusako had returned to my family home in the country to have our baby, and I was planning to join her there later. But then the words came like a bolt from the blue: *Please forgive me.*

It was a long letter. I'd just arrived home from work and stood under the ceiling light to read it, still wearing my raincoat with buttons undone.

I've been wondering and worrying about whether I should tell you this. But now I've just decided to come out with it. You may ask why I haven't mentioned it before. To be honest, it's partly because I was scared. Another reason is that it has nothing to do with our lives together. And I believe that it should have nothing to do with our lives together. But now that I'm about to have your child, I've started feeling very nervous about it. I've become very worried that even if I said nothing and just locked it away in my heart, it might still affect the baby and cause unpleasant memories when he or she is older. I don't want to burden your child with memories like that. These days, whenever the baby moves inside me, my only thought is that I simply must tell the truth to someone as soon as I can, and rid my body of all those lies and unpleasant memories. I almost feel as if I'm being urged on by our unborn child. Of course, you are the only person to whom I can open my heart now. I've been tormenting myself over whether I should tell you about it or not. But I can't hold back any longer. So I've resigned myself to telling you about it now. You'll probably be surprised to hear all this so suddenly, but please let me finish.

And she went on to tell me about her past.

In the summer of the year before we were married, she had had a sordid sexual relationship with another man.

She used to serve as a cashier at a restaurant called Kurumiya, near the publishing company where I once worked. My company used to hold meetings in the restaurant's upstairs room. I myself would go to the restaurant for an inexpensive lunch or a cup of coffee once or twice a week, and, in the process, met my future wife there at the counter. At the time, I was twenty-four and she was twenty.

Once I'd grown fond of her, I stopped going to the restaurant, choosing instead to meet her outside. I proposed to her that summer and we were married in the autumn. She became pregnant almost immediately.

In the summer of the year before we got married, Fusako was nineteen. That was when she had the sordid encounter with a man called Nakaoka, a chef at the restaurant.

I refuse to see that person as myself. I can't bear to think that it was me.

Fusako was a distant relative of the owner of Kurumiya. When she dropped out of part-time high school in her hometown for family reasons, she was offered the cashier position at Kurumiya. Nakaoka was already living in the restaurant at that time. There were four men who worked in the kitchen, as well as ten waitresses. The waitresses all came and went every day, but the men lived in a room next to the kitchen.

Nakaoka was a tall, long-faced, heavy-browed man of around thirty. His reputation as a chef was good, but he was a taciturn, expressionless type. Apart from issuing instructions to the juniors or taking orders from the waitresses with a grunt, he would hardly ever utter a sound or even smile. At first, Fusako found him strange and a little unsettling. Yet she also thought he seemed somehow dependable. What was more, Fusako was the only one that brought out a different side of Nakaoka—he would sometimes say a few short words to her, or smile and flutter his eyes at her, his expression surprisingly kind. Little by little, Fusako found herself increasingly drawn to Nakaoka. The following year, when she turned nineteen, she started to feel, in a vague way, as if she were waiting for something from him.

One evening at the height of the rainy season, Fusako brought the day's takings and cash register receipts to the owner's office after closing time as usual, then went upstairs to check everything. It was the job of the late-shift waitresses to tidy up after closing time, but they sometimes missed things, and so Fusako had agreed to check the restaurant every evening just to make sure.

She was walking around the upstairs room making sure the windows were locked, when suddenly the lights went out. Someone had turned them off.

"Who's there?" Fusako asked. As she turned, she could see a tall man walking briskly toward her through the darkness.

When she realized that it was Nakaoka, Fusako instinctively felt that she'd been waiting for this moment.

"Oh, it's you!" she said, trying not to be afraid. Nakaoka walked around her and suddenly embraced her from behind. Taken completely by surprise, Fusako screamed and shook her shoulders free. Then unexpectedly, in a fraction of a second and as if from nowhere, Nakaoka's hand slid straight down toward her lower abdomen. Fusako gave an involuntary cry and pulled her stomach inward, then found her bottom pressed forward by Nakaoka's rigid thighs.

Nakaoka stubbornly tried to force himself on Fusako. She resisted by bending her body as hard as she could and squeezing her knees firmly together. As the two struggled with each other in this way, Nakaoka suddenly released his grip. Then he slowly backed off and walked out of the room, fortunately without having his way with her.

Though released from her ordeal, Fusako couldn't bring herself to walk away immediately. With her stomach drawn in and her knees held together, she hopped like a rabbit toward the light switch. Her need to brighten the room was greater than her shame at being seen. She switched on the light.

Nakaoka came ambling toward her in a manner that was quite at odds with his attitude a moment earlier. "Tell people if you like," he said, breathing a laugh in her direction. He shook his head as he went back down the stairs.

Fusako's mind was filled with a sense of shame. For now she knew exactly what Nakaoka wanted from her. And it was not what she'd been expecting.

She went straight to the upstairs back room to check herself over. Her elastic was loose, but she was otherwise intact. For that she was relieved.

From that time on, Fusako remained wary of Nakaoka. When she did her rounds after closing time, she always went in the company of her cousin, who was married and lived in the next room. Nakaoka, meanwhile, simply reverted to his former taciturn self. He spoke to Fusako or smiled at her in his usual way, as if he'd completely forgotten his wild behavior of that night. Fusako started to think that perhaps she had misunderstood, and that his behavior had simply been a clumsy way of expressing his feelings. But then she realized that that couldn't be so. If he'd been trying to express his feelings, surely he would have approached her from the front, clumsy or not. Gripping someone by the waist from behind was surely not normal.

In any case, Fusako wished Nakaoka would say something about it. Since he'd done what he'd done without saying a word, she found it hard to understand his intentions.

Two months passed. Then, during the Bon festival in August, the awful day arrived.

The restaurant owner and his wife had taken their children to visit the family grave in a nearby prefecture, while Fusako's cousin and her husband had gone back to their hometown in Shinshu. As a result, the restaurant was temporarily closed. Fusako had stayed behind to look after the premises, together with an old lady who used to help out. The kitchen workers appeared to have left for town earlier that morning.

It happened in broad daylight.

Intending to collect the laundry from the drying area, Fusako had gone along the upstairs corridor to the small access door at the back. Suddenly, she was struck on the side of the head by something hard. She turned instinctively to see Nakaoka looming beside her. As soon as she saw him, her desire to escape fell away, and she simply sank down wearily onto the corridor floor. Her head was spinning and her mind was numb.

Nakaoka dragged Fusako into her cousin's room and ripped her clothes off. He lay heavily on her and forced himself inside her body. Resist as she might, Fusako could summon up no strength to fight. As she struggled with what energy remained, the sash of her cotton kimono became loose, slipped upwards, and began pressing in tightly on her chest. Now she could breathe only with difficulty.

Suddenly Fusako felt a sharp pain piercing through from her inside toward her back. She heaved Nakaoka's heavy body up onto her chest. It all happened in an instant. In the next moment, Nakaoka's body rolled off and collapsed onto the tatami matting beside her. Nakaoka escaped from the room on all fours.

Eventually Fusako managed to sit up. She was in a state of disarray. She hurriedly adjusted her clothing, then squatted there for a moment with arms around her knees and her face turned down. Soon she regained her composure and tremulously started to examine herself. She was bleeding slightly. A little further away, a thick whitish substance oozed stickily down the inside of her thigh. Fusako didn't know what the substance was, but, for some reason, a sense of relief welled up inside her when she saw it. She closed her legs and lay quietly on her side. And for a reason she could not explain, her tears started to flow endlessly.

———————————

Please forgive me. Please believe me. And please forget that I have told you this.

———————————

With that, Fusako closed her letter.

Our child's third birthday arrived.

Our own birthdays simply come and go, but Momoe's could aptly be described as "arriving," approaching from afar and growing closer with each passing day. My wife starts making various mental preparations some days beforehand, but when the day arrives, it's a rather modest affair.

As Momoe's birthday fell on a Saturday, I left work at midday and dropped in to a department store. There I found the doll Fusako had asked me to buy, and took it home with me. The doll was one that could be undressed and bathed, her clothes changed and her blonde hair untied, braided, or combed. On the train home, I found that the doll also cried; she let out a cry every time I shifted my grip on the box, much to my embarrassment. Her cry was amazingly loud.

Fusako placed a birthday cake, topped by three green candles, in the middle of our low dining table. She surrounded it with our child's favorite foods, which she'd taken the trouble to buy, and invited us to sit at the table. Then she lit the three candles with a match.

"Now you have to blow the candles out," she told the child, puckering her lips in imitation of blowing. Momoe looked up at me, then back at the candles as if she had no idea what was going on.

"Go on, give it a try," I said by way of encouragement.

The child closed her eyes and blew at random. That was enough to take one candle out.

"Actually, you should blow them all out in one breath, but if you can't yet, that's all right. Just blow them out one at a time," Fusako said to no one in particular, as if apologizing for the girl.

Momoe's eyes glistened with pride that she could blow even one candle out. So eager was she to blow out another that she nearly burned her nose before she could reach it, and jumped back in fright. It wouldn't have been funny if she'd burned her nose on her birthday. So my wife and I blew out the two remaining candles between us.

"Happy birthday, Momo-chan!"

"Happy birthday!"

The child smiled bashfully as she fingered the doll's tiny wrist.

And that was how Momoe celebrated her third birthday.

I drank two bottles of beer to mark the event. Not being in the habit of drinking at night, I felt the effects immediately.

When nearly everything on the table was finished, it was I who suggested we all go out to the local bathhouse.

"Are you sure you're not too drunk?" said Fusako, even as she started to prepare the bath things.

I have enjoyed going to the public bath ever since I was a child, my wife no less so. These days, since we've become accustomed to living in other people's homes or in plywood-walled apartments, we know just how convenient it is to slip out to the bathhouse, and what a precious time of happy family harmony it offers. Whenever I set out toward the bathhouse chimney, standing tall and slender on the far side of the field, I suddenly feel freer and lighter in my body. My wife also shows renewed vigor in her expression, and becomes unusually talkative. Momoe always wants to run on freely ahead. And something I enjoy in particular is the way the chimney of the bathhouse, which can be seen from a distance, seems to recede toward the far edge of the field when we start walking toward it.

Momoe wanted to take her new doll, the one I'd bought that same day, with her to the bathhouse. Normally, we try to go as lightly burdened as possible, and my wife was going to act out a little scene with the doll to persuade Momoe to let it wait for us at home. Still, since it was her birthday, we decided to let her have her way just this once, but only on condition that she carried the doll herself.

As we stepped out of the apartment, the smoke from a bonfire lingered over the asphalt road in the dim light of dusk.

A little way down the road, the rows of houses ended and the road was lined on both sides with the fresh green of early-summer barley fields. At this point, Momoe seemed to rather regret having brought her doll. Usually, my wife and I each take one of her hands and swing her through the air on the count of three, until we reach the point where the gravel road turns into the field.

"Mummy?"

The child immediately looked up at her mother with an air of dismay.

"What about one-two-three?" she said.

"But you're holding your doll," Fusako replied with deliberate curtness, as if to say *I told you so.* "You can't do it with one hand, can you."

Momoe pulled a sullen face and looked down at the palm of her empty hand.

At that moment, the phrase *And all promenade!* suddenly popped into my head.

It's one of the commands that a folk dance leader calls toward a circle of dancers while clapping a rhythm with his hands. I don't dance myself, but I saw people doing it once.

It was soon after we'd first moved to the apartment, while I was strolling through the neighborhood in my quilted jacket one Sunday.

I had turned off the asphalt road into a side street, and was passing between some old-style farmhouses when I heard the lilting melody of "Oh, Susannah!" coming from the woods ahead of me. Listening more carefully, I could also hear some rhythmic hand-clapping.

Must be folk dancing, I thought. *Maybe there's a park or something in there.*

I quickened my pace a little as I moved toward the forest. There I found, not a park, but a large Western-style building painted green. On a large grassy area in front of it, more than fifty young men and women were folk-dancing to music from a banjo band. The bandleader, clapping a rhythm with his banjo still hanging from his neck, was yelling a string of commands: *And bow!*, *And all promenade!*, putting unusual stress on the final syllables.

The young dancers, both men and women, were all dressed in costumes of different colors and were leaping around with great agility. Their faces were completely wreathed in smiles, and showed not the slightest trace of troublesome bashfulness, meanness of spirit, inhibition, hesitation, or the like. Their smooth, faintly reddened faces were full of honest trust and kind-heartedness.

I crossed my arms inside my quilted jacket and gazed at them from the other side of the fence. *Now that's what I call happy harmony,* I thought. I suppressed my rising sense of envy and went home.

And all promenade! From that time on, those words must have become lodged at the back of my mind. And they returned to me, of themselves, when I felt this moment of happy harmony with my family.

"Hey, let's do *And all promenade!*" I said to Momoe. She looked up at me and smiled.

"With this hand?" she said, holding her empty hand high.

"Of course."

"What about the doll?"

"I'll hold it for you."

She handed her heavy burden to me and jumped up in the air with a laugh of glee.

"What do you mean, *And all promenade*?" asked my wife.

"Don't you know? You hold hands and skip along together."

"Momo-chan can't skip yet."

"Doesn't matter, we'll just pretend."

Strictly speaking, we should have joined both hands, leaned forward in one direction and then skipped along together. But since I was holding Momoe's doll, we would have to make do with just the one hand.

"Come on then," I said, taking Momoe's hand.

"How?"

"Like this."

I clumsily demonstrated a skip, and my wife laughed. Momoe hopped up and down in excitement.

"Are you ready now? All right, here we go. *And—all—promenade*!"

I skipped forward, but the child merely giggled and hopped forward as if taking a running jump.

"*And all promenade*!"

She seemed about to lose her footing, clung on to my hand with both of hers, and remained dangling in that position. From there I lifted her over and carried her forward, calling out "Hey-up!" as I did. When her feet touched the ground, I called "Hey-up!" again and lifted her up once more. It was nothing really—just me single-handedly giving our child a "flying swing," which my wife and I would usually do together. Momoe was now laughing uncontrollably, and after landing back on the ground made no attempt to jump up again. But just when I thought she'd had enough . . . "Again!" she cried.

"All right—hey-up!"

In no time at all, we were racing off together hand in hand.

"Be careful!" I thought I heard my wife's voice call behind us at that moment.

However, fired up by the child's laughter, I had unwittingly started to gather speed as I ran, making Momoe skim low over the ground. Before I knew it, I was running so fast that I began to worry whether it was all right to do so with the child completely suspended in midair.

"Hold on!" I felt a premonition of danger and suddenly slowed my pace. But the danger had already arrived.

Something suddenly hit my shins. At the same moment, my vision went topsy-turvy and I was thrown violently down onto the road. Later I realized that, because I'd reduced my speed so suddenly, Momoe's legs, which had been flying through the air, were carried forward by their own momentum and became entangled in my own. At the time, however, I had no idea what was going on. The only thing I can remember clearly is that the child's body rebounded elastically under my side, and that her eyes, now suddenly beneath mine, abruptly opened very wide in that instant.

That jolted me back to my senses. I had fallen with the child pressed under my armpit, in the style of a judo hold. I was propping my upper body firmly on my elbows, and although it was something I couldn't remember doing, I was glad that I'd thrust them out so quickly. For if I hadn't, I would surely have landed with full force on the Momoe's chest.

I got to my feet. As I did, Fusako came rushing to the scene, and swiftly scooped up the fallen child. She started to strike her violently on the bottom while repeatedly calling her name. Then at last I realized the worst of it. I noticed that Momoe was not crying at all. She was not even uttering a sound. I felt an involuntary shudder and rushed to my wife's side.

I will never forget the look Fusako gave me then.

She turned and glared at me as though I were a complete stranger. The look in her eye was as cold as a knife, unforgiving. Then, suddenly, she grimaced as if about to cry. "It's all right," she screamed before dashing off into the cornfield beside the road, as if to prevent me from taking Momoe from her. As she did, one of her wooden sandals flew off her foot and landed on the asphalt road with a loud clatter.

It's all right—what did that mean? That she could manage on her own? That I needn't bother looking after the child any more?

As I turned the question over in my mind, I retrieved Fusako's sandal, picked up Momoe's doll, and just stood there at the roadside, silently watching my wife as she struck the child's bottom and swirled about as if dancing in the cornfield, causing untold havoc among the drooping ears of barley.

It was not long before a breathless gasp, like the first cry of a newborn baby, issued from the child's mouth.

I had wondered what on earth I would do if she never cried

again, as I often recalled later, an icy shiver going through me each time. I would have crushed my own child, whom I loved so dearly—and just when I was trying to make her happy!

Whenever I look back on it, I see my capacity for causing untold harm with just a single mistake. I'm horrified and feel weak at the knees.

Luckily, Momoe had suffered only a mild sprain of her right ankle. We immediately rushed her to the nearest doctor, who undressed the child and examined her. She lay faceup on the long leather-covered examination table, her back sticking to the surface as if she were in a cold sweat. Each time her hand or foot was raised, a peeling sound could be heard. My main concern was that she might have hit her head, but that appeared not to have been the case. Nor was there any particular damage around her abdomen, which had been pressed downward beneath my weight.

By the time we finally learned that her only injuries were a sprained right ankle and a scrape on her right side, both of our faces were covered in perspiration. This was certainly no time for happy harmony. We returned home without going to the bathhouse.

The scrape healed quickly, but the sprained ankle took much longer to recover. We diligently applied wet compresses, using a concoction the doctor had given us, but it didn't have the slightest effect. I often used to sprain my ankle when I was in junior high school, and when I applied a wet compress of wheat flour dissolved in vinegar, the sprain would heal after only two or three days. Remembering that, I asked Fusako to make the same compress. Perhaps we used too much vinegar, for the sole of the child's foot turned white and swelled up like the grain of tatami matting. We stopped using that compress after two or three days.

This was the second time Momoe had been injured. The first was when she dislocated her right shoulder at the age of two. She was playing by herself, rolling around on the floor in our apartment, when she suddenly started crying. We took her to a doctor and discovered that she had dislocated her shoulder. So she first injured *herself* and then was injured by her father. Perhaps she secretly felt wary not only of herself but also of me from that time on.

This was the second time, too, that my wife had looked at me as though I were a stranger. The first time was soon after she'd given birth to Momoe in my hometown. I had already joined her there, but on the night the child was born, I was not at home. I was in a local bar, drunk and singing songs.

I returned home in the first light of dawn to discover that Fusako had given birth during the night. First of all, I was lambasted by my mother in the hallway.

"What kind of father stays out all night while his first child is being born?" she demanded in a very low voice, the blue veins on her forehead protruding.

I went into the birthing room without saying a word. I sat cross-legged on the floor by the baby's pillow, which had been set down next to my wife. I peered at my own child's face for the first time, and was startled to see that her sleeping face was exactly the same as my own when I was a baby. Of course, I have no way of knowing what my face was like when I slept as a baby.

But the moment I saw my baby's sleeping face, I immediately felt it was exactly the same as my own had been. The likeness was so uncanny that it startled me.

I turned toward Fusako, wanting to compare the baby's sleeping face with hers. I was sure she had been asleep until just a moment before, but was surprised to find that she had opened her eyes wide and was looking at me. Hers were not the eyes of someone who had just woken up, but of someone who had been lying awake for hours. Then I noticed that she was looking at me as if I were a total stranger.

"I've had the baby," she said, quietly but firmly. I merely nodded in silence. "I wanted you to see her first." She suddenly started crying, her shoulders heaving violently. "Why else did I write you that letter? You're heartless, heartless, heartless!"

The child woke up and started to cry.

After reading the letter, I'd passed my remaining work onto others and had rushed to join my wife in a mad panic, leaving everything else unfinished. I wonder if, on seeing her for the first time after receiving the letter, I looked at her as though she were a stranger. Until that moment came, at least, I felt that she'd changed into a completely different person, and was apprehensive about meeting her. But when in fact we met, I felt her even closer to my heart than she had been before.

I told her that she had not been raped. I convinced her that, although she appeared to have been raped, Nakaoka had not completely penetrated her. I told her that there were deviants like him in the world. She said she had more or less suspected such things ever since we were married, but that she resented the existence of a man who had betrayed her so. I shared her resentment, but what I resented more was the fact that Fusako's physical sensation at the time struck a deeper chord with me than her mental reaction did.

I couldn't help questioning her repeatedly about every detail of her ordeal. Each time I did, I felt as though my whole body were rammed full with rods of fire. "Take your clothes off," I would then demand, falling victim to sheer carnal lust.

Wishing she could think me more brutal than Nakaoka, I would stare at her body, now close to full term, then clutch my head in my hands and start to weep. I felt utterly wretched.

From the beginning, it was never a question of forgiving or not forgiving her. I could of course believe what she had told me. But I could not forget about it, try as I might. Her nightmare was like a reel of film playing inside my head. Year by year, the film might turn a little more sluggishly, its image might become less sharp, but still the picture could be seen. Even now, the film sometimes turns of its own accord, triggered by chance events. And once it begins to turn, I have no way to stop it.

When we argue over some trifling issue, for example, the film suddenly starts to turn, whereupon even an argument that was almost finished begins to smolder drearily again. The argument becomes twisted, and I no longer have control of my reason.

Sometimes I find myself suddenly overcome with rage. Even I myself don't know why I'm angry. I can do nothing to stop it. If I'm in bed, I'll suddenly rip off the edge of the quilt. If I'm eating, I break my chopsticks or throw food from my plate.

Even after we had moved to our new apartment, I once

grabbed some deep-fried oysters from my plate and threw them right into my wife's face.

"Why don't you hit me? Please hit me!" she implored. I said nothing, but merely continued throwing oysters at her. They hit her on the cheeks and forehead with a crisp, slapping sound. I could never hit my wife with my own hands. In any case, the walls are made of plywood.

In the autumn we went to a hot-spring resort in Joshu for a two-night break.

When Momoe's ankle showed no sign of improvement, we took her for an X-ray, and were told that she had a hairline fracture on her ankle bone. If we'd left it any longer, we were told, she would have walked with a limp for the rest of her life. For that, I blushed in front of the doctor. Momoe's leg was set in plaster for a while, but by the beginning of autumn she had at last completely recovered.

The two-night trip was our way of celebrating her recovery.

We took a steam train first and then transferred to an electric train. When we arrived, we treated ourselves by taking a taxi to the resort from the station.

Our inn was busy with guests, but once in our room we felt very tranquil. As soon as the maid had left, Fusako stood on tiptoe and quietly tapped the wall.

"It's real!" she declared, then shrugged her shoulders and chuckled.

But before dinner, she returned from the bathroom looking downcast.

"That's odd," she said.

"What is?"

"My period's started. It's not due for ten days yet. That's odd."

We slept quietly for two nights before returning home.

Then, on the second day after our return, there was an unexpected turn of events.

I was about to leave work that day when I was called to the telephone. It was a call from my wife.

"I'm at K. Hospital," she said without ado.

K. Hospital was the largest in our area.

I immediately thought of our child. I thought that perhaps her ankle had suffered a relapse due to the incomplete hot-spring cure.

"Is it Momoe?" I asked, heart in mouth.

"No. It's me this time."

"You? What's the matter?"

"I started bleeding badly at home earlier today."

"Bleeding?"

"You know," she replied, then said nothing. At length I realized what she meant.

"And?"

"I was so shocked that I got someone to call me a taxi here. The doctor said I was on the verge of having a miscarriage."

"What?!" I said in amazement, completely taken aback. "But surely you . . ."

The idea of a miscarriage was bizarre when she wasn't even pregnant.

"Yes, I was surprised to hear it too. It seems I was pregnant without even knowing it. You remember last month, when I said my period was very short? I was already pregnant then, apparently. The doctor said it sometimes happens like that."

"But your period started when we were at the hot spring!"

"No, that was the first stage of a miscarriage. And anyway, I did think it was odd at the time."

"Yes, but . . . how could it have happened?"

"The doctor asked me if I'd done any particularly strenuous work, or been on a long journey recently. When I told him about our trip, he said that must have caused it. He said I shouldn't have let myself be jolted by the train."

I felt somehow indignant at that.

"But how were we to know? We couldn't help it. If we'd known, we would never have gone there in the first place."

"That's right. We couldn't help it."

We both said nothing for a few moments.

The delicate workings of a woman's body are simply beyond me.

"Anyway, what happens now?"

"The doctor says that if I move around too much, I'll start to bleed a lot more, and then I'll miscarry. So it would be safer if I stayed in hospital until things calm down, he says."

"Well, you'd better do that, then."

"But what about Momoe?"

"I'll manage."

How exactly I would manage was something I would think about later. Anyhow, I thought this might be a good chance to patch up my relationship with my daughter.

After saying that I would drop by the hospital, I hung up, immediately left my office, and went straight there. Fusako was in a two-bed ward, lying beneath a summer quilt of a kind I'd never seen before. Her face was pale.

"I'm sorry this had to happen," she said.

"It's all right," I replied. "It's not all your fault."

She forced a smile. In the other bed, a middle-aged patient was facing toward us and sleeping with half-closed eyes. Fusako lowered her voice. "She's had an operation for an ovarian cyst," she said.

I went to see the doctor.

The doctor informed me that the fetus was still partly attached to the placenta, and that there was a fifty-fifty chance of preventing a miscarriage as things stood. There would be some hope if the bleeding stopped now, but if it continued any longer, the fetus would have to be removed by curettage.

"Of course, our first priority is to save the fetus, so I'd want to avoid curettage if at all possible," he added.

I returned to Fusako's bedside and told her what the doctor had said.

"What do you want to do?" I asked.

"The bleeding seems to have stopped . . ."

"Well, do you want to stay in hospital and get ready to have the child?"

"Yes." She looked up and gazed at the ceiling with a serious expression for a few moments.

"Will you be all right?" she asked at length.

"I'll be all right. I'll manage somehow."

She continued to stare at the ceiling without a word. Suddenly, I realized that it was not the cost of having a baby or the effect it would have on our lives that was troubling her, but the question of my own affection.

"I'll be all right," I repeated.

"Yes. I'm sure you will," she said, as if trying to convince herself. Then at last, she looked back at me with an expression of relief.

I decided to go home, but first made a note of the things Fusako needed me to bring.

"Then, if possible, could you bring Momoe with you tomorrow morning?" she added at the end.

"Yes, I'll bring her."

"I want to tell her that she'll be a sister next year."

"She can sleep with me tonight."

Fusako seemed to think I was proud of that. "She needs to go to the toilet once a night, you know," she said with a chuckle.

"I can manage that," I said, getting up to leave.

"Oh, and . . ."

"What?"

"Speaking of going to the toilet . . . That reminds me."

I smiled wryly.

"How do you do it?"

"There's a pot under the bed. Would you mind?"

I took out an enamel pot from under the bed.

"And do I wait while you do it?"

"You do. Sorry."

I had no option but to squat at the foot of the bed, until at length I heard the sound made by my wife under the quilt.

I remembered that there had been a similar scene once before. It was when we visited Fusako's destitute family home in the first winter after we were married. Late one night, as I lay in bed after Fusako had slipped out, I heard the sound of a chamber pot being filled on the other side of a sliding screen. As I recall, it was a clear, sweet sound, like the ringing of a little bell.

If only we could go back to those days, I was thinking.

I suddenly felt like praying.

Perhaps Emi in Number Four has placed a memento of her youth under her bed, and prays to it in the same way.

And if only we could make a fresh start from there!

But that was an impossible wish. Even the sound of the little bell had become nothing but a yellow, frothy sound. We would have to make our fresh start from the here and now, as many times as it took.

I stared in silence at the darkness under the bed, until the sound had stopped.

About the Author

TETSUO MIURA was born in 1931 in Aomori, Japan. After dropping out of Waseda University, he worked for a while as a schoolteacher, but when four of his five siblings committed suicide or ran away, he left teaching behind, fearing that his family carried a curse. He rematriculated at Waseda and began writing. After *Shinobugawa* won the Akutagawa Prize, he pursued writing as a way to purify his "cursed blood," producing a series of novels. His other works include *Umi no michi* (*The Paths of the Sea*), depicting the "red-haired harbor geisha" born to foreign sailors and Japanese mothers; *Shonen sanka* (*Hymn of the Young Men*), describing the young Japanese who traveled to Europe on an official mission in 1582; and *Byakuya o tabisuru hitobito* (*The White-night Travelers*), the tale of a misfortunate family.

About the Translator

ANDREW DRIVER lived in Japan a number of years, working as a freelance translator and as a screenwriter for documentary films. His published translations include *Salmonella Men on Planet Porno* (thirteen short stories by Yasutaka Tsutsui), and a series of works on the Hotsuma Legends of ancient Japan. A British national, he now lives in Oxford, England.